**“I’m blessed to have such good friends. Thanks for helping me out.”**

Nicole considered him a good friend?

Longing stirred in Judd’s gut. He took in the open living space, where her friends were chatting as they unpacked and played with the babies.

He’d never been part of a group.

He wasn’t the group type. Not even this one.

“Hey, Judd, could you give me a hand back here?” Mason called from the master bedroom. “I want to get this bed set up.”

“No problem.” His gaze lingered on Nicole as she went over to check on the babies. She took the tiny girl out of the seat and smothered her with kisses on her cheeks and neck. The baby smiled. Judd did, too.

Being part of Nicole’s group was a one-night-only thing. Otherwise, it would put him in too much contact with her. Then people *would* talk. In a small town like Rendezvous, gossip was inevitable. Hanging around her all the time wouldn’t be good for her reputation.

Besides, he needed his space. Always had. Always would.

**Jill Kemerer** writes novels with love, humor and faith. Besides spoiling her minidachshund and keeping up with her busy kids, Jill reads stacks of books, lives for her morning coffee and gushes over fluffy animals. She resides in Ohio with her husband and two children. Jill loves connecting with readers, so please visit her website, jillkemerer.com, or contact her at PO Box 2802, Whitehouse, OH 43571.

## Books by Jill Kemerer

### Love Inspired

***Wyoming Sweethearts***

*Her Cowboy Till Christmas*
*The Cowboy's Secret*
*The Cowboy's Christmas Blessings*

***Wyoming Cowboys***

*The Rancher's Mistletoe Bride*
*Reunited with the Bull Rider*
*Wyoming Christmas Quadruplets*
*His Wyoming Baby Blessing*

*Small-Town Bachelor*
*Unexpected Family*
*Her Small-Town Romance*
*Yuletide Redemption*
*Hometown Hero's Redemption*

Visit the Author Profile page at Harlequin.com for more titles.

# The Cowboy's Christmas Blessings

## Jill Kemerer

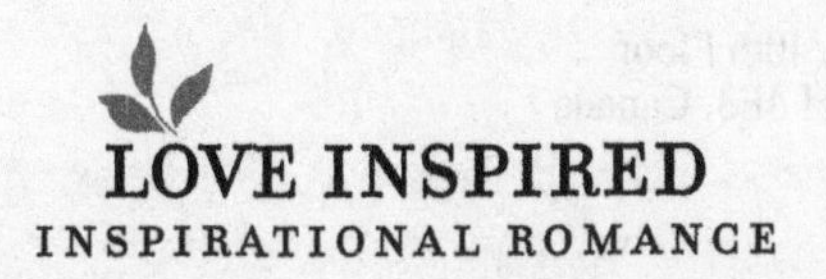

Recycling programs for this product may not exist in your area.

ISBN-13: 978-1-335-42973-5

The Cowboy's Christmas Blessings



This edition published by arrangement with Harlequin Books S.A.

For questions and comments about the quality of this book, please contact us at CustomerService@Harlequin.com.

Love Inspired
22 Adelaide St. West, 40th Floor
Toronto, Ontario M5H 4E3, Canada
www.Harlequin.com

**Printed in U.S.A.**

But my God shall supply all your need
according to his riches in glory by Christ Jesus.
—*Philippians* 4:19

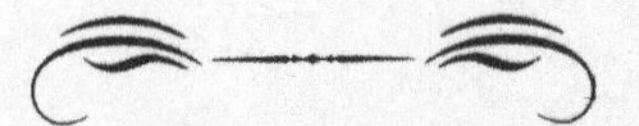

To Mindy Obenhaus.
Your friendship blesses me every day.

# *Chapter One*

Evicted by her own mother right before the holidays. The thought of being homeless with three babies had jumped to the top of Nicole Taylor's worst-case scenario list, and the list had been growing exponentially since her husband, Aaron, passed away last Christmas. Hadn't the year been bad enough?

She needed to find a place to live ASAP.

Nicole steered her minivan north of Rendezvous toward Judd Wilson's ranch. With Thanksgiving only a few days away, she gave a silent prayer of thanks for clear roads. Wyoming could be treacherous this time of year. The miles melted away as Nicole mindlessly took in the snowcapped mountains and horses huddled together in the distance. She hoped the babies were okay. She hadn't been away from her four-month-old triplets, Amelia, Henry and Eli, for more than an hour at a time since they were born. But this was a crisis, and her friends had offered to babysit.

Gabby, Eden and Brittany made it sound so easy: *Talk to Judd. He has a two-bedroom cabin sitting empty on his property. He's rented it out in the past. It's one story—no stairs—perfect for you and the babies.*

Her friends clearly had no idea how intimidating the prospect of asking Judd for a favor was to her.

She was nervous about this meeting for a number of reasons. One, she had no income, only Aaron's life insurance policy, and it needed to stretch until she figured out a way to support herself. A normal job was out of the question. She'd never be able to afford childcare for three infants.

But if she could do something from home, she might be able to get by until the triplets were in school full-time.

Reason number two? She'd never lived on her own before. The past several months staying with her mother and sister, Stella, had been rough, but while Mom wasn't exactly hands-on with the children, her presence had been reassuring. Every time Nicole thought of being solely responsible for the babies, her breathing came in quick gasps and she had to fight the sensation of falling.

And then there was reason number three.

She wouldn't think about three. It was disloyal and wrong and absolutely inappropriate, given that Aaron hadn't been dead a year.

The sign for Judd's ranch appeared, and Nicole navigated her minivan down the rambling driveway. She'd never been here before and wasn't sure what to expect. Empty pastures gave way to a grouping of pines. When the trees cleared, her jaw dropped. The biggest log home she'd ever seen loomed to one side. She parked in front of it. Views of pastures, hills and mountains quieted her troubled heart.

*Lord, give me courage.*

She grabbed her purse and groped around for the diaper bag but came up empty-handed. *Duh!* If she wasn't so jittery, she'd laugh. She didn't need a diaper bag to talk to Judd. Those three tiny babies had completely changed her life, and she thanked God for them every day. In fact, it wouldn't hurt to check on them.

Nicole sent a group text to her friends, and within seconds, her phone dinged. Gabby assured her everything was fine. A picture came through. The six of them had squished together for a selfie. Eden held Amelia, Brittany held Henry, and Gabby held Eli. So adorable.

She stepped out of the vehicle and pulled her shoulders back. As she made her way to the covered porch, she gathered her thoughts. Was the cabin available to rent? If yes, she'd assure Judd she'd be a model tenant. Then she'd offer him an insultingly low amount for it and hope he wouldn't be offended or laugh her off the property.

As if he would. Judd was the nicest guy she'd ever met.

"Hey there," a low voice called from the porch.

And there stood reason number three. Judd Wilson himself. The only guy besides Aaron who'd ever made her insides all fluttery. She wasn't even near Judd, and her nerves were positively crackling.

The rancher was a good ten years older than her, yet something drew her to him. It wasn't his cut muscles, although she'd have to be in a coma not to appreciate them. It certainly wasn't his sparkling personality, given he was the quiet, serious type. It wasn't even the fact he owned a massive, successful ranch and had never been married.

Whatever it was, she needed to ignore it and focus on today's mission: finding an affordable place to live.

"Thanks for agreeing to meet with me."

She climbed the steps and tried to sound cheery.

His deep blue eyes held a gleam as he opened the front door and ushered her inside. His jeans, long-sleeved T-shirt and cowboy boots fit him perfectly. Not that she'd noticed.

She shouldn't notice.

Heat climbed the back of her neck. Why couldn't she look away?

Judd led her to a living room with soaring ceilings, a stacked-stone fireplace, dark leather furniture and views of pastures and distant mountains from the large windows. The house was unbelievable—grand and welcoming at the same time. She caught a glimpse of the kitchen and let out the tiniest sigh. Even from here, she could see the pretty cabinets and granite countertops. A girl could bake up a storm in there.

"Do you want me to take your coat?" he asked.

"Oh, no, I won't be staying long." Her

palms grew clammy. She wasn't ready to do this.

She loathed asking for favors. Disliked owing anyone anything. Her entire life she'd been dependent on the generosity of other people. Just once she wanted to be independent, to not have to rely on anyone else.

"Is something wrong with the babies?" He took a seat on a leather chair and gestured for her to sit on the couch.

"No, they're fine." She sat, keeping her purse on her lap, and forced herself to swallow her pride. "Actually, I heard you have a cabin on your property you rent out sometimes."

"I do."

"I also heard no one is living in it at the moment." She tightened her grip on the purse straps.

"Correct."

"Well, Mom and her boyfriend, Steve, are moving to Florida." It wasn't the first time her mother had fallen head over heels and decided to move in with a guy.

It probably wouldn't be the last. "It's all really sudden. Basically, they're hitting the road after Thanksgiving and, with her lease expiring at the end of the month, she gave her landlord notice."

"She's kicking you out?" He sounded dumbfounded, the same as she'd been two days ago when her mom had told her.

"Yeah." Was her face on fire?

"The cabin's empty." Judd stood. "I'll get the key and take you over. I don't know if it's what you're looking for, but you're welcome to it."

The fluttery feeling came back full force. His generosity made him very, very attractive.

He disappeared into the kitchen, then came back holding up a key. "Come on. I'll take you over."

As she followed him through a mudroom, then outdoors and down a side porch, the next problem loomed: How was she going to approach the topic of rent? Her checkbook might as well have a neon sign flashing I've Got Nothing.

She'd done the math dozens of times since Aaron died, and the life insurance had to last until she produced a reliable income. Thankfully, Mom hadn't expected help with utilities or rent, but basic items like formula and diapers for three babies still cost a fortune.

As soon as Nicole got her housing situation locked down, she had to figure out how to make some money. What could she do, though? She didn't have a college degree—just years of experience working at a bakery.

Judd opened the door to a multivehicle garage and waited for her to enter before closing the door behind them. With a push of a button, one of the garage doors opened.

"We can take the UTV." He pointed to one. "The cabin's not far."

She climbed into the passenger side of the off-road vehicle and tried not to notice how close Judd's arm was to hers as he started it up. He'd grabbed a jacket on the way out of the house, and it only served to make him look more rugged, more capable than usual.

Her feminine core—the one she'd assumed no longer existed—gave a sigh of pleasure at all the masculine strength next to her.

She should be ashamed of herself. Was this what loneliness did to a person? Made them hyperaware of any eligible guy who showed them a sliver of kindness?

The UTV burst forward, and she lunged for the handle. Crisp air chased away her thoughts as they drove down a gravel path surrounded by evergreen trees. Soon they stopped in front of a cute log cabin. It had a small lawn in the front, and the back was guarded by tall dark green pines. A stone chimney climbed the side, and the covered front porch had three railing sections made of logs forming Xs. Stone pavers marked a path from the driveway to the porch.

"Was this dropped down from a fairy tale?" She climbed out and headed toward the pavers. "It's adorable."

"It's been remodeled. A storm damaged it a couple of years ago. Aunt Gretchen helped me pick out everything." He unlocked the front door and waited for her to enter. "Want me to stay out here?"

"No, of course not."

As soon as they entered, she relaxed. The open living space was small but bright, cozy and updated. Her gaze was instantly drawn to the kitchen to her left. The white cabinets and laminate countertops looked new. Everything was laid out with care. A large refrigerator, gas oven, double sink, dishwasher and hardwood floors made her want to pinch herself. It was perfect.

"The bedrooms and bathroom are back here." He strode down the hall, his cowboy boots clicking on the floor.

Both bedrooms were large, and the bathroom met her needs.

"What's in here?" She pointed to the door at the end of the hall.

"Utility room." He opened the door.

She peeked inside, where a washer and

dryer, washtub, hot-water tank and furnace were housed. Plenty big enough for her to do laundry. A window revealed a view of the backyard, and a door led out to it.

As they returned to the living room, her heart began to pound. How on earth was she going to suggest Judd rent this beautiful cabin to her for next to nothing?

She'd spent enough time around him over the past eleven months to want to protect their friendship. They usually sat together at social functions, although he never stayed long. Unlike most people, he didn't pepper her with awkward questions or look at her with pity. He simply accepted her. His easy silence was a welcome change from years of being married to a talkative extrovert. It was also a nice reprieve from being treated like a trauma patient around town.

"So, Judd, this cabin—" she spun in a slow circle before meeting his eyes "—is perfect. I would love to rent it from you."

"Good. Here." He handed her the key.

"Wait—not so fast." She frowned. Didn't he want to discuss the particulars? "About the rent…"

He rubbed his chin with a confused look in his eyes. "Rent? I'm not taking any rent from you."

His words should have filled her with relief, but they didn't. When would she ever stand on her own two feet? Would she always be a charity case?

The fact Judd made the offer didn't surprise her as much as it should have. The cowboy was… Well, he was too good to be true.

"That's very kind of you—" she lowered her chin "—but I have to pay you something."

"Keep your money. Use it for the babies." Judd knew it wasn't smart, offering free use of the cabin to the one woman he actually felt comfortable around, but she needed it. And he wanted to help. He wasn't a fool—she had no job and getting one would be pointless if she had to pay a babysitter to watch three babies. As it was, he had no idea how she managed to look so calm and capable raising triplets.

Every Sunday morning, he watched Nicole navigate her way through the church parking lot with the babies strapped into a triple stroller. Her friends always helped her into the church as soon as they spotted her. There was no way she could live in a place with stairs, that was for sure. His cabin would make life easier for her.

"I can pay you, but I can't afford much." Her long blond hair, sage-green eyes, full lips and pale skin gave her a natural beauty, and he'd scolded himself more than once since she'd moved back to town to stop ogling her like some kind of creep. For crying out loud, he was at least ten years older than her!

"I told you, I'm not taking your money." He sounded gruffer than he intended. Nicole might be a mom of three and a widow, but she had pride. Then again, so did he, and he wasn't budging.

"Judd," she said, sighing. He liked the

sound of his name on her lips. "It's too much."

Had she misconstrued his intentions? His face grew warm. "Doesn't the Bible say something about taking care of widows and orphans?"

"Yes." Her sweet, shy smile reminded him why he always ended up near her at social functions. There was no pressure to converse, but when they did talk, it felt natural.

Making small talk had never been easy for him.

"Is the furniture okay?" he asked. The couches Aunt Gretchen had picked out were a little feminine for his liking, but the dining table was good and solid.

"It's perfect, but we haven't worked out the rent yet." Her eyes shimmered with uncertainty. "I can pay you a little bit each month. When I start earning an income—"

"You got a job?" He crossed his arms over his chest. How would she manage that?

"No, but I'll find a way to support myself. Maybe something part-time. From home." Her back was straight, her chin high, but he couldn't help thinking she looked as fragile as one of the china dolls in Aunt Gretchen's living room cabinet.

She sneezed. "Excuse me for a second." With her finger under her nose, she hurried down the hall to the bathroom.

Money had never been an issue for him. He'd grown up in Boston with parents who had plush government jobs. His mom and dad loved to socialize. Judd hated it. His parents hadn't known what to do with an introverted kid who was bored at school and refused to participate in sports. The final straw had been when he'd told them he was skipping college and moving to Wyoming to ranch with Uncle Gus. They still hadn't gotten over it.

It had been the best decision he'd ever made. And he owed it to his late uncle to secure the ranch's future. Judd needed to make sure it would be in good hands if anything happened to him. But who would appreciate the property and cattle the way he did?

No one came to mind. He wasn't close enough to anyone to name them as beneficiary in his will. He needed to figure it out, soon. He wanted it done before the new year came around. All he had to do was look at Nicole, still in her midtwenties, who'd already lost a husband. People could die at any time. Including him.

When Judd asked Aunt Gretchen for advice, she'd suggested, as she always did, he get married and have children. As much as he'd like a partner to grow old with and a few kids to raise, he didn't see it happening. He was too quiet, and his two previous relationships had ended badly. Both women had claimed he was too reserved and they couldn't read his mind.

Had he ever asked them to? Judd almost shook his head. He didn't get women and they didn't get him. Never had. Never would.

"Sorry." Nicole came back, patting her nose with a tissue. "Now, where were we?"

"The furniture." He swept his arm across the room. "Do you need me to move any of it out?"

She hesitated. "After Aaron died, I gave away our living room furniture. We'd gotten it secondhand from his parents, and it had seen better days. The dining table was damaged in the move, so I got rid of it, too. My bedroom set and all my other stuff is in storage."

"I'll clear out the furniture from both bedrooms." He'd ask Dallas and Clay, his two full-time ranch hands, to help him haul it out to his pole barn tomorrow.

"You don't have to do that. I don't want to be any trouble."

He almost laughed at the thought of her being trouble. If anything, she'd saved him from trouble. For almost twenty years he'd dreaded every social event this town expected him to attend...until January, when she'd arrived. She made the events bearable.

It wasn't a romantic thing, though.

She was a widow. With three babies.

And way too young for him.

Romance was out of the question.

"Let me know when you want to move in," he said. "I'll help load and unload your stuff."

"Judd..." There it was, his name again. The hairs on his arms rose. Maybe this wasn't a good idea. She'd be living here in the cabin. Close by. And she was real pretty.

No big deal. He'd spend his days the way he had since he'd turned eighteen. Riding around the ranch. Not hanging out with Nicole Taylor and her cute little triplets.

"Don't say you'd be imposing," he said. "The cabin's empty. And I'm always out taking care of cattle and the ranch. You won't even know I'm here."

Her eyes flickered with hope.

Why was he holding his breath waiting for her answer? He had no stake in this. It would be better for him if she didn't live here. He didn't like complications, didn't do relationships anymore.

"I don't feel right not paying you." Her frail voice did him in.

There was no way he was taking a cent from her. No. Way.

"Here. It's yours. I won't take your money." He shoved the key into her hand. He wasn't letting her or those babies go homeless. His uncle Gus had taught him better than that.

Nicole stared at the key in her palm. The metal was warm from Judd's hand. The warmth was nothing compared to the heat blasting her heart, though. Of all the generous things people had done for her since Aaron's death, this was the kindest.

She scrambled to figure out a way forward. Part of her was terribly thankful he didn't want her money, but the other part balked at paying nothing. He'd made it clear he wouldn't accept rent. There had to be some way she could repay him.

And shouldn't they at least discuss this arrangement before she moved in?

"What if you need the cabin? Didn't you say it was for guests?" She curled her fingers around the key, not wanting him to change his mind but knowing these questions had to be asked.

"I never have guests."

"What if you do?"

"My house is plenty big enough for anyone who'd want to stay."

She couldn't argue with that. Still…

"Okay, but let's say someone else comes along, someone who could actually pay you rent. Would you give me a couple weeks' notice so I could find something else?" She hated the thought of moving in and later being forced out. It was better to know the expectations right off the bat.

"It's yours." His eyes were dark blue, like the sky right before dusk. "I wouldn't kick you out. My income is from the ranch, not from renting out this cabin."

"I'd need to move in soon—really soon." She bit her bottom lip. Her mom had put her in a bind. If Nicole had been given more time, this process wouldn't be so stressful.

"You can move in today if you want."

Today. A thrill of excitement sped down her spine. She was going to have her own place! Her own bedroom. Her own kitchen. No more tiptoeing around Mom's or Stella's needs.

But today was too soon. If he cleared out the bedroom furniture tomorrow, she could technically move in on Tuesday. Maybe her friends wouldn't mind skipping their weekly support group session to help her move in. She didn't have a ton of stuff. The babies had been sharing a bedroom with her at Mom's place, so it wouldn't take long to pack up. Everything else was in storage. It would be a relief to not have to pay those fees anymore.

Judd was helping her more than he knew. How could she make it up to him?

The one thing she prided herself on was her cooking, especially baking. She'd barely cooked or baked since last December, when Aaron's respiratory infection turned out to be a lung complication from Becker muscular dystrophy. They'd both thought he'd live until middle age, but he'd developed pneumonia and died on Christmas Day.

She missed cooking and baking. She missed the simple things in her old life.

Her old life was over.

It was time to create a new one, and living in this cabin would be a good start.

"I'll cook supper for you," she blurted out.

"What?" Was that fear in his eyes?

"Yes, I'll make you supper." The idea grew as she spoke. She might not have a lot to offer, but she knew what cowboys in these parts liked to eat. "Stop by in the evening and I'll have a meal ready for you."

"It's not necessary."

"I'm a fine cook." Nicole raised her chin. "And I'm an even better baker. You won't take rent, and I won't live here without giving you something. So, please, take my food. Cooking is the one thing I'm good at."

"You're good at a lot of things." His voice was husky and his cheeks grew red.

His words softened the brittle edges of her doubts about herself. Maybe she wasn't as helpless as she felt. A fresh beginning might make the raw panic she'd been pushing away for so long go away for good.

"What time do you usually eat?" she asked.

"It's too much." He shook his head. "You've got the babies. You don't have time for all that."

"I'll make time for it." Saying the words out loud filled her with the sense of purpose missing since Aaron died. She could do this. The triplets had recently begun sleeping through the night, giving her more energy during the day.

"It doesn't feel right." He stood with his legs wide.

"Feels right to me."

He studied her. His jaw tightened. Finally, he nodded. "Not every day, though. You need a break."

"I really don't."

"No weekends and that includes Fridays. You should relax."

Relax? The thought was laughable. She had no idea how to relax anymore, and with three babies, she didn't have time to, anyhow.

"Monday through Thursday. You can stop by at six. Deal?" She held out her hand.

He stared at it for a few seconds. Then he shook it. "Deal."

Finally, something was going right in her life. She had a free place to live. A great little cabin to call her own. Now she just had to get through Christmas and the anniversary of Aaron's death without falling apart. Then life would go on as usual.

# Chapter Two

Late Tuesday afternoon, Judd loosened the straps holding down the crib in the bed of his truck. Mason Fanning and Dylan Kingsley had been helping him move Nicole's items from storage and her mom's house to the cabin all afternoon. This was the final item. Her friends Eden Page; Mason's wife, Brittany; and Dylan's fiancée, Gabby Stover, were inside helping her unpack. The cold wind brushed his cheeks as he let down the tailgate. What if people talked about Nicole living on his ranch?

There was nothing to talk about. She was a grieving widow with triplet babies, and no one would realistically pair her with him even if she wasn't.

"Let me help." Dylan hopped up on the bed of the truck and grasped an end of the crib. Together, they lowered it to the ground. Dylan worked as a ranch hand for Stu Miller and was marrying Gabby in the spring. Judd thought highly of the unpretentious cowboy.

As they carried the crib to the front porch, Gabby held the door open for them. She owned the local inn and always went out of her way to include Judd in social activities, whether he wanted to go or not. The way her eyes lit up for Dylan, well, Judd wouldn't mind if a woman looked at him like that. Inside, he caught a glimpse of Nicole laughing as she held one of the triplets. He quickly glanced away.

He and Dylan managed to get the crib down the hall and into the bedroom with little fuss. The other two cribs, a changing table and a long dresser were crammed into the room. Boxes were piled along a wall. The sound of feminine chatter, occasional chuckles and baby noises drifted from the living area.

"Is that it?" Mason leaned his forearms on either side of the doorway. He owned a cattle ranch near Rendezvous and had married Brittany Green earlier this year. Ever since the wedding, Mason had gotten more involved in the community. Wife or not, Judd didn't see himself ever being more active in the community. Socializing had never been his strong suit. He didn't know what to say, and sitting around gabbing felt like a waste of time, anyway. He had a ranch to run.

"Yeah, that's it." Judd led the way back to the living room. Eden Page was strapping one of the babies into a seat. Eden was single and not dating anyone. Like Judd, she was reserved, which should have made them ideal for each other, but he wasn't feeling it. He liked Eden; he just didn't *like* Eden. He assumed the feeling was mutual.

One of the babies let out a cry. Gabby tossed a pacifier to Eden, who gave it to the little guy. Judd took in the boxes and piles of unpacked items yet to find a place. There was a lot left to do before this cabin would get organized. At least Nicole and Brittany had moved to the kitchen, where they were putting away plates.

He paused a moment to get a good look at the babies. They all had wispy brown hair, big eyes and chubby cheeks. The little girl was the smallest and quietest. The two boys were kicking their feet, blowing spit bubbles and making cute sounds. His attention returned to the girl. So tiny, staring up and watching the world.

Funny how he had the urge to scoop her up and protect her. Something told him the boys would be roughhousing and wanting to ride horses as soon as they could walk. He smiled just thinking about it.

He'd never been around babies much. He'd certainly never held one or even noticed them, really. And here he was, thinking about kids who weren't even his own. He hoped Nicole living here wouldn't turn him into a softy.

Aunt Gretchen's suggestion about having a wife and family came to mind. If he had children, he'd be able to show them the importance of the ranch. He'd train them to respect the land and cattle. Then he wouldn't worry about this place being in good hands when he got old. Lately, he'd been waking up in the middle of the night, troubled about what would happen to it if he died. What if it was sold to be developed? Or split into smaller parcels?

This vast property was meant for raising cattle. It would break his heart to think of it used for anything else.

"Is that all right with you, Judd?" Nicole had meandered over. What was she saying?

"I'm sorry. I didn't hear you." Her delicate perfume—light and sweet, the same as the woman who wore it—drifted to him.

"Dylan and Gabby are going to run to town and get pizzas for us."

"Oh, right." He should leave. These were her friends. He got along fine with them, but he didn't want to cramp her style. "I'll leave you to it."

"What? No." Her forehead wrinkled as she shook her head. "You're eating with us. Did you think I wanted you to leave?"

Actually, he did think it, and he wasn't sure why. Default assumption, he guessed.

"I'd be upset if you didn't stay. After all you've done—moving my stuff and clearing out the rooms earlier…"

Were her eyes getting teary or was he imagining it? She seemed emotional. He shifted from one foot to the other. He'd never been good with female emotions.

"It was nothing. I'm happy to help out." Moving her stuff was easy, and she acted like he'd saved the day. He hadn't realized how much his assistance meant to her.

"Thank you." She sniffed. Her eyes were definitely watery.

"Are you okay?" Why had he asked her that? He knew better than to ask women if they were okay. The question only encouraged them to share a wagonload of emotions he couldn't handle. It typically meant several minutes of them expressing their feelings and him trying to decipher what they were talking about. His last girlfriend, Josie, came to mind. He'd liked her. Tried to understand where she was coming from. And she'd accused him of being cold and unreachable before she'd slammed out of his life.

He still had no clue what he'd done wrong.

"I'm fine." Nicole looked away. "New chapter in my life, that's all."

Yeah, it was a new chapter in her life, and he felt bad about it. He'd never known her husband. Nicole and Aaron had been so much younger than him. They'd married and moved out of state right after graduating from high school. Talk around town was Aaron had been charismatic and well liked. When he was a teenager, he was diagnosed with some disease—Judd couldn't remember what—and the town rallied around him, hosting wild-game dinners to help with his medical expenses.

Judd was under no illusions. Nicole had

lost her soul mate, the love of her life, when Aaron died.

"I'm sorry," he said. "I know this must be rough."

She placed her hand on his sleeve, and the contact surprised him. Her eyes glistened with gratitude. "I'm blessed to have such good friends. Thanks for helping me out."

She considered him a good friend?

Longing stirred in his gut. He took in the open living space with her friends chatting as they unpacked and played with the babies.

He'd never been part of a group.

He wasn't the group type. Not even this one.

"Hey, Judd, could you give me a hand back here?" Mason called from the master bedroom. "I want to get this bed set up."

"No problem." His gaze lingered on Nicole as she went over to check on the babies. She took the tiny girl out of the seat and smothered her with kisses on her cheeks and neck. The baby smiled. Judd did, too.

Being part of Nicole's group was a one-night-only thing. Otherwise, it would put him in too much contact with her. Then people *would* talk. In a small town like Rendezvous, gossip was inevitable. Hanging around her all the time wouldn't be good for her reputation.

Besides, he needed his space. Always had. Always would.

"Thanks again for everything." Nicole stood in the doorway as her friends left. The crescent moon in the black sky seemed too tired to give off much light. She knew the feeling. Judd had been the first to leave. He'd eaten a few pizza slices and been on his way. She'd wanted to convince him to stay longer, but she hadn't dared. He'd been so helpful, and it had been nice to lean on him.

Leaning on him wasn't something she should get used to, though. She didn't want to wear out her welcome. She needed this cabin too much to jeopardize their arrangement.

She closed the door. Every light in the cabin was on. It was just her and the babies. Tonight would be the first time she'd be sleeping in a bedroom by herself since they were born. It would also be the first night she had no other adult nearby to help if something went wrong. Not that anything would, but…

What if she couldn't do this—raise the triplets—on her own? Her breathing grew shallow, and the scary hollowness she'd lived with after Aaron died threatened to return.

Closing her eyes, she tried to regulate her breathing. Her grief counselor, Mrs. Reeves, always told her to think of the scary hollowness like being in a stairwell with steps descending into darkness. If she chose to go down them, she'd be surrounded by darkness and fear. But the stairwell also had a side door with a glowing exit sign above it. If she opened the door, it led to sunshine and healthy triplets and moving forward in confidence.

She had a choice—take the stairs down to paralyzing fear or go out the side door and focus on the good things in her life.

It had given her a way to cope through the terrible days after Aaron's death. Just because he'd died didn't mean her reality was a place of pitch-black darkness. Good things still existed. She'd focus on them. All three of them were in the living room at the moment.

Eli and Henry were getting fussy; the babies always did this time of the night. She went to the kitchen and prepared three bottles, then returned and knelt on the floor, pulling the boys' seats closer to her so she could feed them at the same time.

"Today was quite the day for my big boys, wasn't it?" she cooed. "We're not living with Granny anymore. It's just us."

*Just us.* A pit formed in her stomach.

She was now completely responsible for these tiny beings.

*Take the side door, Nicole.*

"We're going to be fine. We've got a great place to live and friends who are here for us if we need help." Eden, especially, had lent Nicole a hand more and more over the past month since moving in to the apartment above Brittany's dance studio. "You'll be in your beds tonight and Sissy will be in there, too. It'll be the same as Granny's, except quieter."

Much quieter. This move might be a blessing in disguise. Mom and Steve often watched television until late at night, when he'd finally go home. And Stella was always slamming doors in the wee hours of the morning. Who knew where she'd been? Although the triplets had recently started sleeping through the night, Nicole never got uninterrupted sleep, and it was mostly because of her living arrangement.

But she wasn't complaining. Mom had taken her in and given her a home all year. What would Nicole have done without her?

Her cell phone rang. Nicole tapped it

then set it to speakerphone to keep her hands free. "Hello?"

"How did the move go?" Mom sounded frazzled. She and Steve had been packing his house all day.

"It went well. Everything's in my new place. I haven't made much of a dent in unpacking, though."

"Wish I could help you, but we're on a tight deadline. We'll be leaving Wyoming right after Thanksgiving dinner. The U-Haul is bursting."

"I'm going to miss you, Mom."

"Me, too, honey. But you and the kiddos can come visit us anytime. I can't wait to get down there and wear shorts every day. Steve found tennis courts near our apartment. I might learn how to play."

"Sounds great." Except it didn't. Mom's relationships never lasted more than a year or two. "Did Stella get her stuff over to Misty's?"

"That's part of the reason I'm calling." Was Nicole imagining the restraint in Mom's tone? "Your sister called earlier.

Looks like she was offered an opportunity she can't pass up."

"What are you talking about?" Prickly sensations covered her skin. Stella had always been headstrong and flirty. She'd matured some since working for Gabby at the inn for the past several months, but Stella hadn't taken Mom's news about relocating well.

"Seems she got a job offer at a hotel in Vancouver. The owner really likes her. She's coming home tonight, packing up and heading out."

"She'll be here for Thanksgiving, though, right?" Nicole couldn't believe it. Her sister was moving away, too? "Wait. Does Gabby know? Don't tell me Stella's leaving the inn without giving notice."

"You know your sister."

That was code for yes, her sister was leaving without giving Gabby any notice.

A tension headache formed behind Nicole's forehead. She'd specifically asked Gabby to hire Stella as a favor, and now her dingbat of a sister was going to leave her in the lurch.

"Did Judd help you move or was it just your other friends?" Mom asked.

"He helped."

"Good. Now that you're living on his ranch, you should spend as much time as possible with him. None of the other girls around here have snagged him. Here's your chance. You're a pretty girl, Nicki. Use it to your advantage. He's one of the most eligible bachelors in town."

She cringed, not daring to form a reply. Sometimes it boggled her mind how her mom's brain worked. The thought of *snagging* Judd for security gave her a terrible icky feeling.

"Don't unpack everything," Mom said. "Who knows? If you're smart, you could move in to his big house."

"My hands are too full to think about getting married again, Mom."

"Well, moving in could lead to marriage. You've got three babies and no income."

Nicole wiped her finger over her eyebrow, praying for patience. As much as she loved her mom, she never, ever wanted to grow up to be like her. "I don't think so."

"Beggars can't be choosers." Her mom yawned. "I'm beat. I'll see you at the Riverview Lounge on Thanksgiving. One o'clock."

"I thought we planned on four o'clock."

"We moved it to one. Steve wants to get in as many miles as possible before it gets dark."

She had so many questions, so many things to say, but what was the point? "Okay, see you at one."

Her mom ended the call.

This was why Nicole had latched on to Aaron as a kid. She'd never been able to rely on her parents. Her mom changed plans on an hourly basis. Her father had left them when Stella was a toddler, and he'd only shown up once or twice a year until moving to the East Coast a few years later. Since then, Mom had clung to any man who would give her the time of day.

What if Judd got the impression Nicole was trying to snag him the way Mom suggested?

She shook away the awful thought and turned her attention to the boys. She'd have to be careful not to give Judd that impression. After burping and snuggling Henry, then Eli, she gave them their Binkies. Then she unstrapped Amelia, brought her over to the couch and fed her, too.

"And how are you, my tiny princess?" Amelia stared up with shining eyes that seemed to see into Nicole's soul. "You're never as hungry as your brothers, are you?"

Nicole tried not to be concerned about Amelia's smaller size. The doctor assured her she was gaining weight and would likely be petite her whole life. But it was difficult not to worry when Amelia was so itty-bitty compared to the boys.

"Guess what, sweetheart?" She caressed

her tiny head. "We're living on our own again." Nicole would be surrounded by her things and in charge of her days. No more sharing a bathroom with Mom and Stella. No more trying to quiet the babies at 6:00 a.m. so her mother could sleep.

She could follow any schedule she wanted because she didn't have to answer to anybody else.

Her throat tightened uncomfortably.

She'd never wanted to be alone. And now she was. The thought almost choked her.

Amelia gripped a section of her long hair and was bunching it in her fist. Nicole took a deep breath. She wasn't alone, not really, and it wasn't only the babies keeping her company.

Gabby and Eden had told her time and again at their support group meetings that she could trust God. Her expectations didn't always line up with His will, though. She'd never understand how God could let Aaron die while she was pregnant with three babies. She'd needed him. And he was gone.

*I don't have to know all the whys, Lord. You're always with me. I'll cling to that.*

For the next hour, Nicole played with the triplets before changing them one more time. Soon they were sleeping in their cribs, and instead of doing the smart thing and going to bed, she padded to her room, changed into sweats and opened the first box stacked against the wall. She had no idea what was in it. Last January she'd packed her apartment in a haste without labeling the boxes. Aaron's death and the pregnancy had left her barely functioning.

She peered inside. Aaron's basketball trophies from high school. It was as if she was sitting on the bleachers in Rendezvous High's gym waiting to cheer him on all over again. It had been their sophomore year when he began complaining of cramping in his legs. The basketball coach had gotten on him about his lack of stamina. Aaron had responded by training harder. Nicole hadn't worried much about it. He was invincible. A basketball star. The hometown hero. Everyone loved him, and she'd been his biggest fan.

They'd been inseparable since second grade, when he'd stopped Jeff Borland from pushing her on the playground. She didn't know if it was possible to fall in love at eight years old, but she was pretty sure she had. Their junior year, when Aaron's legs got weak and the cramping intensified, his parents took him to see doctors. The diagnosis was devastating—Becker muscular dystrophy.

At first it had felt like a death sentence, but after running tests on everything from his heart to his lungs, the doctors had assured Aaron he'd likely live to middle age or beyond. Nicole could still remember collapsing in his arms with relief when he'd told her his prognosis.

Not wanting to waste a minute, they'd married the summer after graduating from high school. His senior year of college, they'd decided to start a family. They hadn't been successful. Two years later, she'd gone on fertility drugs. And then last year…

If she'd known she'd be a widow with triplets, would she have done anything differently?

Did she have any regrets?

Nicole put the trophy back and closed the box. She'd loved Aaron, but their marriage hadn't been perfect. From third grade on, he'd called the shots, and she'd happily tagged along. Aaron had a larger-than-life personality. He loved to talk and talk…and talk.

She'd been the captive audience of the Aaron Taylor show most of her life.

He was the one who got a full-ride scholarship and earned a business degree while she worked at a bakery to help pay for their expenses. But later, while he was finding success at work, she was losing her voice in their relationship, and she'd never had much of one to begin with.

This year without him had been eye-opening. After months of grief and all the sessions with Mrs. Reeves, Nicole realized she missed Aaron, but she didn't miss the dynamics of their relationship.

Sighing, she stood up, pressed her hand to her aching back and then carried the box out to the hall. She'd save the trophies for the kids. They'd want to see their daddy's prizes someday. And she'd tell them all about his basketball days here in Rendezvous.

Turning on the light of the utility room, she glimpsed something streak across the floor. The box fell out of her hands and she jumped back, shrieking.

A mouse!

Her pulse raced so fast, she thought she might pass out. Slamming the door shut, she turned, raced to her bedroom and grabbed her cell phone with fumbling fingers. Quickly, she found Judd's number.

He picked up on the first ring. "What's wrong?"

"It's in there!"

"What?" He sounded confused.

"There's a mouse in the house!" Oh,

dear, she sounded like Dr. Seuss. "It's running around the laundry room!"

If there was one mouse, there could be two, and if there were two, there could be entire families. What if the walls were full of them?

"I'll be right there." The line went dead.

Taking deep breaths, she used her phone's flashlight feature to check on the triplets. Thankfully, her scream hadn't woken them up. She hustled to the living room and turned on the porch light.

*Come on, Judd. Get here!*

What if he didn't live a hop, skip and a jump away? What would she have done then?

It didn't matter. He did live within arm's reach, and she couldn't be more thankful. Because she was not ready to be on her own if it meant dealing with mice by herself.

A mouse? Judd thrust his arms into a jacket, pulled on his boots, grabbed his hat and went outside. He was used to seeing mice in the stables, but Nicole sounded terrified.

Must be a girl thing.

The wind picked up as he strode down the lane to her cabin, so he tucked his chin into the collar of his jacket.

When Nicole called, he'd just gotten off the phone with Aunt Gretchen. He called her every night. She lived alone in town, and he wouldn't be able to sleep not knowing if she was okay. His aunt had turned seventy this year.

Aunt Gretchen was the sister of his dad and Uncle Gus. Her husband had died a few years before Judd arrived in Rendezvous as an awkward, withdrawn teenager. She always thought the best of Judd. As time went on, he depended on her for advice and her unwavering support, and he helped her out whenever she needed anything. She acted like he was the son she never had. He was closer to her than anyone.

How much longer would Aunt Gretchen be around?

An owl hooted as the cabin came into view. The front windows glowed in cheery welcome. No one else lived nearby. One of his full-time ranch hands had a house five miles away. The other stayed in a cabin on the east side of Judd's property. The arrangement suited him fine. The men, both single, could take care of themselves.

But Nicole and the babies… She had her hands full and needed all the help she could get. He picked up his pace and rapped on the front door.

Nicole opened it. Her hair was in a messy ponytail, and she'd changed into gray sweatpants and an oversize pink sweatshirt. She looked even prettier and more vulnerable than she had before.

"Oh, thank you. Come in!" She pulled him by the hand and dragged him down the hall.

Her fingers in his hand chased all logical thoughts out of his head. The same protective feeling he'd had earlier when he'd stared at her baby girl flooded him. This woman needed him. It might only be to get rid of a mouse, but she needed him all the same.

"It's in there." She pointed to the closed door leading to the utility room. Then she took a few steps backward with her hands over her heart. Her eyes were as big as the plates she'd unpacked earlier.

"Stay back," he said. "I've got this."

"Oh, I'm staying back. You couldn't pay me to go in there."

He almost chuckled as he slipped inside the room. A box with a couple of plastic trophies blocked the path. He nudged it to the side with his foot. He grabbed the broom he kept on a rack behind the door and crouched down to figure out where the critter went.

There it was. In the corner. He opened the door leading to the backyard then poked the broom at the mouse, causing it to race ahead straight toward the door. With one swipe, he brushed it outside, shut the door and locked it.

After putting away the broom, he opened the door. "All clear."

She'd wrapped her arms around her waist. "Are you sure? What if it has a wife and family? What if there are babies in the walls? Mice could be everywhere." Her voice rose in panic.

"I don't think mice get married."

"You know what I mean." Her deadpan look made him tuck his lips under to avoid laughing.

"I'll get some traps in here tomorrow. In the meantime, I think you'll be okay."

She chewed on one of her fingernails. He doubted she'd sleep a wink.

"Why don't I check the house before I go?" He took a step toward her. She was more petite up close. A good six inches shorter than him.

"Would you?" The breathy quality in her voice spoke to the masculine side of him that relished hauling hay and roping calves and working with his hands.

Yeah, he'd gladly go on a mouse hunt for her.

He nodded and moved toward her bedroom, hesitating before entering. "Is it okay if I go in?"

"Yes, do your thing." She beamed. "I won't be able to sleep if you don't."

He wanted to say something, to reassure her, but he never had the right words, so he merely went into her room and looked along the baseboards. No signs of any mice. He scouted the living room with her at his heels and checked the rest of the cabin, minus the babies' room since they both agreed it would be best not to wake them.

"I'm guessing the mouse sneaked in yesterday while we were moving the furniture out." Now that his duty was done, he'd better not linger. He headed toward the front door. "I'll get traps tomorrow in case he brought a friend."

Her lips had pursed into a cute little heart shape. "Thank you. You must think I'm silly. I really appreciate you coming over."

"I don't think you're silly." He wanted to say more, to tell her she didn't need to worry, he'd gladly stop by anytime she was scared. But the words stuck in his throat. He opened the door and stepped outside.

"Bye." She wore a wistful half smile and shivered in the door frame. "Thanks again."

"Sleep tight." He shoved his hands in his pockets and strode toward home.

Nicole and her babies felt like his responsibility, the same way the animals on his property were, the same way Aunt Gretchen was.

He might not be good with words, but he'd been born to protect. If Nicole needed him for anything, he'd be there. No questions asked.

Crushing his hat tighter on his head, he strode down the path. He thought back on their agreement. Starting next Monday, he'd be picking up his supper from her. He had to admit home-cooked meals sounded better than the frozen dinners he'd relied on for years. It would also give him a chance to check on her, make sure she and the babies were okay. It wasn't like he had to eat with her or anything. She'd hand him a plate and he'd be on his way. No big deal.

But something whispered inside him that it was a big deal.

What was done was done. Nothing he could do about it now.

# *Chapter Three*

The following Monday evening at six o'clock sharp, Nicole wiped her hands on a dish towel and surveyed the table. She'd fed the babies before cooking supper, then lined them up in their seats right outside the kitchen so she could safely keep an eye on them. Tonight's menu? Country-fried steaks, corn and mashed potatoes with gravy. With pop music playing, she'd lost herself in the delight of cooking, only stopping twice to give Henry his stuffed doggy and Amelia her pacifier. Now the food was on the table along with two place settings. It was her first night feeding Judd. He should be here any minute.

She hoped he wouldn't mind eating with her. The past week had been on the lonely side. Her mom and Steve had driven out of Rendezvous right after Thanksgiving dinner. Gretchen Sable, Judd's aunt, had stopped by on Saturday to chat and play with the babies. She'd taken one look at Nicole and insisted on organizing her retired friends from church to come in for a few hours each morning, starting tomorrow, to help with the triplets. Knowing someone would be there to help out for a while each day had taken a huge weight off her shoulders.

Nicole found the salt and pepper shakers in the cupboard and brought them over to the table. Had Judd forgotten about their arrangement? She checked her phone—6:05 p.m. She'd wait five more minutes. If he wasn't here by then, she'd text him.

She'd been looking forward to this meal far more than she cared to admit.

It was understandable, she supposed. Yesterday, Eden and Gabby had babysat for her so she could get groceries, but other than that, Nicole had been alone, and the lack of adult conversation was getting to her.

Meeting the babies' needs every day was like running a marathon. Poor Eli had a runny nose, making him cranky, and Amelia had fussed a lot, too. Nicole was surprised they weren't crying now.

*Knock knock.* Anticipation added a bounce to her step as she went to the door and let Judd inside. He shook his hat free of snow and stomped his boots before entering.

"Come in. The food is on the table." Funny how the sight of him chased away her exhaustion. It was going to be nice to have someone to share a meal with again.

"Oh, uh…" Judd frowned as he stared at the dining area.

"What?" He wasn't backing out or anything, was he? His cheeks were ruddy from the cold. The crinkles around his eyes made him look mature, attractive. A sudden flush of warmth flooded her cheeks. Her reaction was unwelcome, confusing. She wasn't used to being affected by a man.

"I don't want to bother you." He stood rigidly with his hat in his hands. "I could take a plate home."

Why would he think he'd bother her? She was the one who'd offered to cook.

"It's no bother." She waved him over to the table. "Sit down before it gets cold."

He shifted from one foot to the other, still clutching the rim of his hat. *Please, please don't leave.* She held her breath. Maybe what he'd meant was that he was bothered at the thought of eating with her. Did she make him uncomfortable?

One of the babies let out a cry. She went over to the trio in their seats. Eli was reaching for a stuffed rattle, so she placed it in his hand. His sweet little face melted her. She smoothed his forehead before sitting at the table.

Moments later, Judd took off his coat, hung it on a hook on the wall and joined her.

"You didn't need to do all this on account of me." He sat and scooted his chair closer to the table.

"I love to cook. I've missed it." She folded her hands. "Should we pray?"

He nodded. After the table prayer, Nicole dished out the food and they both dug in.

He carefully cut a piece of the country-fried steak and popped it into his mouth. "Mmm…this is good. Really good. Wow."

"I haven't been in the kitchen much since Aaron died." The gravy could use a little salt. She shook some on it and shoved the shaker his way. "Mom was nice enough to cook so I could take care of the babies. But now that they're sleeping through the night, I have more energy."

He chewed slowly, then took a drink of water. The silence pinged her nerves.

"In fact, it felt great to prepare the meal on my own today. Living with Mom and Stella was a bit chaotic." *Chaotic* was an understatement. She'd tried to avoid their tiffs and Mom's giddy attitude concerning Steve, but the close quarters had made it impossible. "Gabby and Eden babysat for me yesterday so I could get groceries. I think I bought out the store." Was she babbling? Why wasn't he saying anything? "How was your Thanksgiving, by the way?"

"Good." He seemed to be enjoying the food, at least.

She wasn't used to quiet meals. Aaron had always launched into a full and very detailed description of his day. And Stella and Mom either gossiped or argued their way through suppers. Nicole took a small bite of the mashed potatoes and peeked at him. "How did you celebrate it?"

"I ate at Aunt Gretchen's and came home to check on a few heifers."

"Are they okay?" She had no idea what a heifer was but figured it was some sort of cow.

He nodded, adding more gravy to his potatoes. "A dose of penicillin cured one. The other was fine."

"How did you know something was wrong?" She pictured a cow lying on its side, moaning. To say she didn't know much about ranching or cattle was an understatement.

"Gut instinct." His deep blue eyes met hers. "I watch them every day. I can tell when something's off."

"What are the signs? I mean, is it obvious when one is sick?" Spending every minute with the triplets had honed her gut instincts, too. She could tell when something wasn't quite right with the babies.

"They weren't eating as much. The one I gave the penicillin to had runny eyes."

Eli started to fuss, so she checked on him. His face was red and he looked ready to wail. She tried to detect what was wrong. Probably miserable from his cold. As Nicole looked around for his Binky, Amelia joined the fussing. Eli's pacifier peeked out from behind his neck.

"Here you go, sweetie," she said, putting it back into his mouth. He quieted down, but Amelia got louder. Nicole tried giving her a pacifier, too, but her baby girl wasn't having it. Nicole didn't want Judd's meal to be ruined by a crying child, so she took Amelia out of the seat and sat with her tucked in her arm.

"Sorry about that." Nicole glanced over at Henry and Eli. They were content—for the moment. "What were you saying?"

He watched Amelia, his expression softening. "What are their names again?"

"This snuggle bunny is Amelia, and the two peanuts down there are Henry and Eli."

"How are you managing?"

"Good. Managing good." It wasn't a lie, not really. For some reason, she couldn't bear for him to think she wasn't capable. No one would call her supermom, but she was doing the best she could. Getting the babies on a schedule had been the smartest thing she'd ever done, but it still felt like she was barely treading water most days.

Cooking tonight had been the first time she'd felt like herself in over a year.

"Are you getting ready for Christmas?" She picked at the food on her plate. Why had she mentioned Christmas? The holiday held no joy for her. Not after last year. She'd spent half of December in the ICU with Aaron. She'd prayed night and day for God to save him when his condition declined, but on Christmas Day she'd returned to their apartment a widow.

"Not yet." The twinkle in his eyes made him look younger. "I'll get a tree soon."

A tree. The corn turned to rubber in her mouth. Two of her bakery coworkers had taken down her Christmas decorations the day before the funeral. After they'd left, she'd thrown every box of decorations in the dumpster.

"I want to get Aunt Gretchen something special this year," he said. "But I'm not the best gift giver."

Good, a distraction. Coming up with a gift for Gretchen would get her mind back to the present, where it belonged.

"I love your aunt. I can't tell you how many casseroles she's brought over or how many times she's stopped by to spend a few hours with me and the triplets since they were born. She's even organizing some of the church ladies to help me out weekday mornings."

"Sounds like Aunt Gretch." His grin revealed the slight gap between his two front teeth. Nicole was used to seeing his serious side—although his eyes often glimmered with humor—but she hadn't been prepared for his full-on smile. The man was gorgeous. He gestured to her. "Do you have any ideas?"

"Well, what does she like?" She ignored the wound-up sensation in her chest.

"Um..." He lifted his shoulder in a helpless shrug. "I've gotten her sweaters, candles and chocolates. I don't want to do the same old thing. She's done so much for me, and she's getting older."

A man who cared for his aunt was a good man indeed. What could he get Gretchen that would be meaningful?

"What about perfume? They have nice sets with lotion this time of year."

He shook his head. "Done it."

"She likes tea." Nicole shifted Amelia to her other arm. "What about a gift basket?"

"Lois and Ada from church usually get her one."

Eli let out a cry, startling Henry, who also began crying. Amelia, meanwhile, sat content as could be in her arms. Nicole quickly sized up the situation. She'd have to put Amelia back in the seat to take care of the boys. As she lowered the girl, Amelia stiffened and began to cry, too.

Well, this was great. All three babies wailing at once.

A tap on her arm made her turn.

"I'll take her. You handle the boys." Judd held his hands out for Amelia, and Nicole froze. This man—this strong, quiet cowboy—was willing to help her with the babies?

"You don't mind?" She lifted Amelia to him.

"Not at all." He cradled the baby in his arms. Amelia quieted instantly and stared up at him in fascination. Nicole didn't waste any time taking Henry out of his seat and, holding him tightly, picked up Eli, too. Then she sat again, with a boy in each arm. Henry quieted right down, but Eli let out a few half-hearted squawks before relaxing. Her little guys needed some cuddle time.

Across the table, Judd was smiling so tenderly down at Amelia that Nicole fought sudden tears.

Thoughts of Aaron pierced her heart. She had to do something before she made a fool of herself. "I'll be right back."

Carrying the boys, she went to their room to put a lid on her emotions.

What if Aaron had lived? Would he have been a good daddy? What would her life be like?

It wouldn't be surrounded with uncertainty the way it was now.

But it didn't mean it would be perfect.

She refused to create some fantasy where if Aaron had lived her life would be free of trouble. She knew better. Life was messy with or without him.

And Judd was patiently taking care of

Amelia out in the dining room, so she'd better stop dwelling on the past and get out there before he thought she was taking advantage of him.

Nicole set Henry in his crib so she could change Eli's diaper. Then she switched babies and made sure both were clean and fresh. Sweeping up both boys in her arms, she kissed each of their foreheads as she made her way back to the table.

Judd was talking in a low, melodious voice to Amelia, his captive audience. He glanced up as Nicole approached, and his eyes darkened into something appreciative. The way he stared at her was…new. Not even Aaron had looked at her like that. It made her feel feminine and capable. Interesting.

"You make it look easy." His gaze swept to the boys.

"Yeah, right." She shook her head. "This house runs on coffee and pacifiers."

"Well, we'd better keep you stocked up on both."

A vision of Judd bringing her coffee and

pacifiers every day lightened her heart. She'd been putting one foot in front of the other for so long, she hadn't had time to dwell on her performance as a mom. The fact Judd thought she was doing a good job meant a lot to her.

He shifted as if he was preparing to leave, but she wasn't ready for him to go. Not yet. How could she prolong his stay?

"Speaking of coffee. Do you have time for a decaf?" Had she hidden the desperation in her tone? She didn't want to be alone again so soon.

He gulped, looking like a caged animal. Then he glanced down at Amelia. "I guess."

After setting the boys back in their seats, she rounded the counter to start the coffee. He needed a Christmas gift idea for Gretchen. She could think about that—it was safe. Scooping the coffee grounds into the filter, she reviewed his aunt's tastes.

Before the babies were born, Nicole had visited Gretchen a few times. A framed picture of a two-story Victorian house, complete with white porch railings and intricate moldings, was mounted on her entry wall. Gretchen had told her about the lovely home she'd grown up in and how much she missed it.

"Hey, Judd?" Nicole turned to face the dining area. A row of cabinets separated her from the table.

"Yeah?"

"I might have the perfect gift for your aunt."

"What is it?"

"You know the Victorian house she grew up in?"

"I do. I see it every time I go over there." Amelia's hand was wrapped around his finger. Once more, Nicole's heart squeezed. He continued. "She has fond memories of her childhood."

"What if we made her a gingerbread house?"

Confusion clouded his features. "What do you mean?"

"A replica of her childhood home." She

filled the carafe with water and turned the machine on. Visions of drawing up plans for the house, baking the structure, assembling it and decorating it danced in her mind. For years her favorite part of November had been creating gingerbread houses for the bakery's store window. Her boss, Delia Roth, had insisted on making elaborate scenes to bring holiday cheer to the community. Delia had shown Nicole all her secrets and had given her more responsibility as time went on.

Yes, making a gingerbread house was one blast from her past she didn't need to push away. She would truly enjoy making the house for Judd's sweet aunt. If he'd let her.

"I don't think so." He shook his head. This evening had not gone as he'd expected, starting when he'd arrived. Instead of a wrapped plate with a *here you go,* she'd invited him in to the very picture of domesticity. Then she'd gone and served him the most delicious meal he'd eaten in a long time, including Thanksgiving dinner.

Now here he was, a baby in his arms, watching beautiful Nicole Taylor pull mugs out of the cupboard as if he belonged here. He never should have agreed to coffee. Or to stay for dinner. And why in Wyoming had he picked up the baby?

He checked Amelia, so warm and content in his arms. Holding her was sweeter than a fudge cake with chocolate frosting. He'd better not get used to it.

"You don't think it's a good idea." She turned to grab a carton of creamer out of the fridge.

"It's not that."

"Then what is it?"

"I'm no baker."

"Well, I am." She rounded the counter and came over to set the cream and a bowl of sugar on the table. "I worked at a bakery after I got married. I loved it. I'm a certified baker and certified decorator."

"Uh..." He rubbed his chin. What now? He couldn't ask her to make a gingerbread house. He had no idea how she was keeping up with three babies as it was. Her confidence in holding two babies at the same time was still blowing his mind. "I want the gift to come from me."

"It will," she said. He couldn't tear his gaze away from her big smile. "I'll help you."

Help him? He could *not* spend even more time with her. "You've got your hands full."

"You do, too." Her teasing tone relaxed the tension in his neck. His hands *were* full at the moment, in the best possible way. Amelia was precious. Who knew holding a baby could feel so nice?

Nicole cocked her head to the side. "You helped me out. Let me help you."

Ahh...this was her way of repaying him for the cabin. She brought two steaming mugs of coffee to the table and set one in front of him before returning to her seat.

"Want me to take her?" she asked.

He didn't, but he also didn't trust himself to drink a hot beverage while the little girl was in his arms, so he nodded. Nicole came over and took the baby from him. His eyes locked on her bare hands.

No ring.

His brain could not travel this road. She was a grieving widow. With three infants. Living on his property. And so much younger than him. Where was his head at?

She gave Amelia a pacifier and placed her into the seat next to the boys. "If you get a copy of the photo for me, I can sketch the house's dimensions and come up with a plan for the structure." Her face glowed as she talked. Man, she was pretty.

He pictured a replica of Aunt Gretchen's childhood home. His aunt would love it. No, she'd more than love it. She'd probably blubber for an hour at his thoughtfulness.

The gift would be special. Meaningful.

Maybe he should take Nicole up on her offer.

But he was already locked in to eating supper with the beautiful mom four nights a week.

Could he handle all this together time?

He'd been a bachelor his entire life. This

eating together and talking about their day and having coffee and holding babies? It was all new. Foreign.

And tempting.

He glanced at Nicole, who had a dreamy expression on her face as she sipped her coffee.

Maybe he was making a big deal out of nothing. If he agreed to make this gingerbread house with her, it would only be a day of his life. No harm could come from that, right?

"Okay, I'm in."

"Really?" Nicole set down the mug, her insides all aglow. "This is going to be so great. I'll get the plans going, and we'll bake the walls and roof first. Let me know what days would be good for you. Then I'll pipe the decorative details on the house before we assemble it. It will have to firm up before we decorate it with the candies and such. Oh, and I know just the ones to make the house beautiful. I think we should go with a pale-pink-and-mint-green theme. Gretchen will love it."

She wished she had a pad of paper to write down her thoughts. Her notepads were in one of the boxes stacked against the wall. She knew herself, though—once an idea about a gingerbread house gelled, it would stay in her mind.

Judd hadn't said anything, so she glanced his way. Creases had grown in his forehead.

"What's wrong?" she asked.

"Nothing. I didn't realize it would be so time-consuming."

Right. He didn't want to spend his free time baking with her. Could she blame him? They hadn't made it through dinner without her having to deal with the children multiple times. He probably thought he'd be stuck carrying a kid around while simultaneously trying to whip up gingerbread walls.

"I shouldn't have assumed..." She pasted on her brightest smile. "I'll bake everything."

"No, no, I want to be part of it." The look on his face screamed otherwise.

"I've been making gingerbread houses professionally for years. I've got this. You take care of your cattle." The letdown she was experiencing grew to ridiculous proportions. She'd liked the idea of them making the house together. Doing it alone would be a challenge.

"And how will you do that with these little ones?" He leaned forward, resting his elbows on the table.

She gulped. She had no idea how, but if she'd been able to fix supper tonight, she'd find a way to bake gingerbread, too.

"We'll do it together." His tone was final.

*Together. Phew!*

"What are you doing next weekend?" she asked.

"Looks like I'm making gingerbread." The twinkle in his eyes made her tummy flip.

Judd Wilson was a good man. A handsome man.

Maybe spending all this time with him wasn't so smart.

Her heart had been mangled and left for dead a year ago. She'd mourned for months. The babies had been helping her heal—well, as much as her heart could be healed at this point. But it didn't mean she was in any shape to have feelings for another man. It wouldn't be appropriate. It might never be appropriate.

Oh, sweet mercy, she was being overly dramatic. This was a gingerbread house—a gift for a kind woman—nothing more. And if Nicole happened to enjoy Judd's company, what would it hurt? Nothing would come of it.

She was a widow with three babies. He was a mature bachelor with a ranch to run.

Besides, making this gingerbread house with him would help her get through Christmas. She needed a distraction from the one-year anniversary of Aaron's death. Then the new year would arrive, and she'd be one step closer to putting the grief behind her for good.

If there was anything she didn't need to worry about, it was falling for Judd Wilson.

# Chapter Four

Tuesday evening, Judd blew dust off the photo albums in his study. He rarely took anything off the study's shelves, since most of the books and mementos had been his uncle's. But Nicole had asked him to find pictures of Gretchen's childhood home so she could design the gingerbread house, and Judd figured he'd find them in here. After his uncle died a few years back, Aunt Gretchen had helped him go through his belongings. They'd kept useful and sentimental items and donated the rest. But the study, well, Judd hadn't wanted to disturb it. It reminded him of pleasant chats and feeling as if he actually belonged for once. He missed his uncle more than he cared to admit.

Carrying the stack of albums to the large oak desk, Judd fought a pang of loneliness. Supper with Nicole the past two days had been enjoyable, not to mention delicious. Usually when he was around other people, it made him feel like he didn't fit in. However, Nicole set him at ease, and he liked helping out with the babies. Amelia, especially. The little girl had wriggled her way into his heart.

He turned the pages of the top album. The bell-bottoms, mustaches and faded colors in the photographs told him this album was from the wrong decade. Uncle Gus had several pictures of the pretty Victorian two-story home he and Gretchen and Dad grew up in, but they were from the fifties. Judd skimmed through the next album, pausing at several pictures with Gus on horseback working cattle.

*I hope I can be half the man you were.* His uncle had taught him to appreciate the terrain and all its vegetation, the animals who made it their home and the four seasons that determined if the herd would thrive or merely survive.

Judd loved every inch of the land passed down to him. He wanted someone else to appreciate it the same way. Then he wouldn't have to worry about what would happen to it when he was no longer around.

No sense dwelling on it now. Wasn't he supposed to be finding pictures for Nicole?

On page two of the third album was a picture of Judd and his parents in front of a Christmas tree. He recognized his childhood home in Boston. His parents were grinning for the camera, but his own face lacked the brightness of theirs. How old would he have been? Ten? Eleven? A rush of memories came back of his parents getting dressed up for parties night after night from Thanksgiving until New Year's while he spent the evenings watching Christmas movies with whichever babysitter they could scrounge up.

It had been a lonely childhood.

He'd always wanted life to be like it was in those movies. Christmas made every problem disappear. The people always ended up surrounded by their loved ones, with thoughtful presents, laughter and hearts full of cheer.

Judd was still waiting for a Christmas like that.

Swiveling in the chair, he stared out the window, where snowflakes drifted past. Maybe he should call Mom. He'd been toying with the idea of visiting his parents for a few days between Christmas and New Year's Eve. Last year he'd wanted to come out for a week in the summer, but they'd gotten a last-minute invitation to spend a month out of the country.

Before he could talk himself out of it, he picked up his phone and pressed his mom's cell number. As it rang, he absentmindedly leafed through the photo albums.

"You won't believe what I'm surrounded with." She sounded breathless and annoyed. She must be stressed about something. She wasn't one to rattle easily.

"Hi, Mom."

"Hello to you, too." A muffled sound came through the line. "Sorry, Judd, I'm in the middle of picking out kitchen decor."

"I thought you had the kitchen redone last year." She was always remodeling one room or another. Maybe he'd gotten it mixed up, though.

"I did." She sounded exasperated. "This is for the condo."

"What condo?"

"You know, the condo. The one we bought in Saint Thomas."

"Saint Thomas?" He tapped his fingers on the plastic-covered page of the album. His childhood feeling of being on the outside looking in came back full force. "As in the island?"

His mom's laugh tinkled. "Of course. Where else would it be? Linda and Jim invited us down this summer, and we loved their place so much, we bought one of our own."

"Are you selling the house?"

"No, no, of course not. We're just sick and tired of winter. You should see the turquoise water and white-sand beaches. The views are breathtaking. I was sure I told you."

This wasn't the first time his mother was sure she'd told him something major. A few years ago, he'd called her out on it—told her it bothered him that she and his dad never let him in on their plans. She'd sighed and said it wasn't their intention to hurt him; they simply forgot to call. He'd gritted his teeth and said she could text him. She'd agreed.

But nothing had changed.

It never would.

There was no sense getting all bent out of shape about it.

"It's a good thing I called now, I guess." He rubbed his chin. The timing might work out in his favor. "I want to come out and visit you guys for a few days after Christmas."

"After Christmas? That won't work. We're flying to Saint Thomas next week. I've been in a packing frenzy. We won't be back in Boston until April."

It was as if a swoosh of cold air froze his lungs.

Shot down. As usual.

"Okay, well, I could fly to your new place, I guess." He raked his fingers through his hair. He didn't want to. Had no desire to book a flight and find his passport and flit around the island with his go-go-go parents. But besides Gretchen, they were the only family he had.

"We're going to be very busy. The contractor is almost finished with the remodel, and as soon as we're settled, we're island-hopping for a few weeks. Then Linda is booking us a cruise in January."

It shouldn't aggravate him, knowing they were happy to spend the holidays with anyone but their son. It wasn't as if this was something new. But it still hurt.

"When did you decide all this?" he asked.

"The cruise? I don't have the details yet."

"No, the condo."

"Oh, let's see—" she made a clucking sound with her tongue "—September. Or was it October? Gary, when did we buy the condo?"

"Beginning of October," his dad yelled in the background. "Are we still on for the Remington Christmas party tomorrow night? Joe asked if we're going."

"Yes, of course. I picked up your suit from the dry cleaners this morning."

Judd raised his eyebrows as his parents went back and forth about beating the rush-hour traffic. Ending this call would be best for his blood pressure. "Mom?"

"Yes?"

"I love you. Text me a few pictures when you get to Saint Thomas, okay?"

"We will. Love you, too." She ended the call.

Judd tossed the phone onto the desk and

resumed looking through the album. The ache in his chest grew. All these years later and he still wanted that Christmas-movie ending. But he didn't know why he kept thinking his parents would be part of it. They had their own life without him. They always had.

Sitting back, he closed his eyes briefly and massaged the back of his neck.

He had to stop wanting something that wasn't going to happen. His parents weren't going to change. They loved him. They just didn't need him.

Shaking his head, he forced himself to concentrate. The last album contained the pictures of the house he was looking for. He carefully slipped them out of the plastic sleeves, pausing a moment to study each photo. There was a view of the Victorian house with flowers lining the side, another angle from the driveway showing off the long covered porch with a white railing and two rocking chairs, and three additional photos of the front of the house with all the intricate molding and woodwork.

In the last one, Gus, Gretchen and his dad, Gary, sat on the top step. Gus was smiling and wore jeans and a T-shirt. He looked to be about fourteen. Gretchen, too, looked happy and wore a dress cinched at the waist that flared out past her knees. Her curled hair was pulled back with a thin headband. She must have been about ten. Then there was Gary, the baby of the family. His outfit matched his older brother's, but he'd propped both elbows on his knees and rested his chin on his fists in a pout.

For a moment, Judd felt sorry for his dad. His energetic, restless personality was nothing like Gus's or Gretchen's. Maybe he'd felt like a misfit, too.

Judd went over to put the photo albums back on the shelf.

Looked like he'd be staying right here in Rendezvous for the holidays. Thankfully, he had Aunt Gretchen. She never made him feel like an afterthought. If he didn't call her, she called him. Knowing he could spend his holidays with her more than made up for his parents not wanting him around.

Making the gingerbread house with Nicole was a small price to pay for his aunt's happiness.

Where were her half-sheet pans? Nicole got on her knees to search through the unpacked boxes in her bedroom Wednesday afternoon. She'd found her stand mixer, cookie cutters, rolling pins, pie plates and a huge assortment of sprinkles in boxes in the living room, but she owned a dozen half-sheet pans and couldn't seem to find them. The pans were vital to baking the gingerbread walls.

What other tools and ingredients was she missing? She needed to figure it out before they got started.

She couldn't wait to begin. In fact, she hadn't felt this hopeful and good in... well...years.

Years? Could it be true?

The hopeful feeling probably wouldn't last, but for now, she'd cling tight to it.

Lois Dern had arrived this morning and stayed until lunchtime to help with the triplets. Gretchen was coming on Tuesdays and Thursdays, and she'd lined up a retired librarian to come on Mondays and another lady on Fridays. They all planned on staying from nine until noon.

Having the extra hands in the mornings gave Nicole the energy she needed to get through the day. Plus, she appreciated the insights Lois and Gretchen shared about life and babies and relying on the Lord.

Nicole unfolded the flaps of another box. A neatly folded tablecloth greeted her. She held it up and set it aside. It had been a wedding gift from Aaron's grandmother. It had been used precisely once, on their first anniversary. Funny how six months ago the sight of the tablecloth would have crushed her. But now it simply held the hint of a memory from her past.

Which reminded her—she needed to call her in-laws later. Nicole had called them on Thanksgiving to let them know she'd moved, and at least once a week, she texted them pictures of the babies. Lance and Sherry Taylor had been good to her. In some ways they'd been part of her family most of her life. Several years ago, they'd moved to Oklahoma to help Aaron's two sisters with their children.

What else did this box hold? Hot pads and old dish towels were jammed in there, and underneath those?

The half-sheet pans! She took them out and hugged them to her. She'd made so many different recipes with them. Scones and cakes and bars and cookies. The pans were like old friends.

Noises crackled through the baby monitor. Frowning, she hoisted herself to a standing position. She'd wasted precious nap time to find her pans, and she still had to make the chili so it could simmer awhile before Judd came over tonight.

Padding into the babies' room, she inhaled the smell of fresh diapers and baby lotion. The best smells in the world, well, besides coffee or a chocolate cake in the oven. Eli was kicking, and one of his socks had come off. His face scrunched as if he was getting ready to wail.

Nicole picked him up and took him to the living room. His legs kept making jerking movements as he fussed. It wasn't time for his bottle—she kept to a strict schedule—so she tried to give him his pacifier, but he spit it out. His face turned red, and he let out a sharp cry.

"Do you have a tummy ache?" She crouched down on the floor and placed him on his stomach. He lifted his head and grunted, his face growing even redder. He let out another cry. "Well, that doesn't look comfortable."

Picking him back up, she bounced him gently as she cradled him to her. Eli was the gassiest of the three, and sometimes moving him around helped. She kissed the top of his head, thankful her babies were healthy. She couldn't imagine how hard it would be if any of them had been born with disabilities or had colic. In fact, she'd been shocked when she'd carried them almost to term.

As Eli calmed, he nestled his cheek into her chest, and she didn't have the heart to put him back in his crib. She looked around the living room. Opened boxes were everywhere. The place looked a wreck.

She really should put Eli back to bed, but a wave of tiredness hit her, so instead, she sat on the couch and turned on the television. A Christmas commercial showed a woman reaching up to place a bulb on a tree while a man looked at her adoringly. Her heart pinched.

It all looked so festive.

So fun.

So romantic.

Real life wasn't like that.

Real life was when a husband complained about the cookie-cutter ornaments his wife bought, calling them childish. Real life was him coming home the next day with expensive blue and silver bulbs because they were *classy*. Real life was worrying she wasn't good enough in his mind anymore since she had no goals beyond raising a family and baking delicious treats. Real life was praying a baby would bring them closer but fearing the worst—that Aaron had fallen out of love with her a long time ago.

She clicked the television off and took Eli back to his crib. It wasn't fair to mentally dump on Aaron. He was gone and couldn't even defend himself, and he'd been a good friend to her all her life.

They'd married young and, as they grew older, they both changed.

Maybe the babies *would* have brought them closer together. She'd never know, and she didn't need to waste time thinking about it.

As she slowly lowered Eli to his crib, Amelia began to squirm in hers.

Nicole held her breath and tiptoed out of the room. *Please don't wake up!* Once she was safely in the hall, she closed the door and hurried to the kitchen to start the chili. The ground beef sizzled in the pan as she chopped onions and green peppers. With one ear trained on the baby monitor, she let out a sigh of relief when several minutes passed in silence.

Stirring the meat, she mentally made a list of the gingerbread supplies. She'd found a roll of chart paper to create the wall templates. A box of disposable piping bags sat on the counter along with her rolling pin. She didn't have any of the ingredients for the actual walls or royal icing, though.

After adding everything to the ground beef, she gave the pot a stir, turned it down to simmer and found a pad of paper and a pen. Sitting on the couch, she started jotting her supply list.

Just then Amelia started crying.

She sighed. Never a dull moment with triplets.

She set the paper down. Her list would have to wait. The babies called.

"I found the pictures." Judd placed the envelope on Nicole's counter when he arrived for supper. She was sorting through a drawer, so he crouched before the babies in their seats.

"Hey there, cutie." He gently shook Amelia's toes covered in fuzzy pink socks. She stuck her little tongue out, then grinned. Glancing over his shoulder, he called to Nicole. "She smiled at me."

"Did she?" Looking flustered, Nicole held a ladle in one hand and a saltshaker in the other. "She must like you. She doesn't smile for just anyone."

He chuckled, turning to Henry. Henry had darker hair than Eli, so Judd found it easy to tell them apart. "How are you, big man? I think you gained a pound overnight." The baby blinked at him. Judd turned his attention to Eli on the end. "And, Eli, does your hand taste good?" The child was trying to eat the outside of his fist.

Judd pressed his hands against his knees to stand up.

"We're all set." Nicole brushed her hair behind her ear and took a seat at the table. The bags under her eyes worried him.

Was she getting sick? Or was she overtired? He sat opposite her.

She folded her hands and lifted her eyebrows for him to say grace. He obliged, and soon they were both blowing on spoons full of piping hot chili. Delicious, as all her meals were.

"You're doing too much." He discreetly glanced her way.

"Nope." She shook her head. "I haven't felt this good in a long, long time. I found most of my baking supplies today."

The gingerbread house. Guilt trickled into his veins like the drip from an IV. "I don't want you wearing yourself out on my account."

"Wearing myself out? Hardly. Lois Dern spent all morning helping me with the babies. She had a lot to say about Misty Sandpiper flirting with some local cowboys. And Gretchen came yesterday. They're amazing."

"But that's only the mornings. Until now you've had help round the clock." He took another bite of the chili and held back a groan. The woman could cook. If it wasn't so hot, he'd have gobbled the contents of his bowl.

"What are you talking about?" She gave him a strange look.

"When you lived with your mom and sister."

"Oh..." She tapped her mouth with a napkin. "I wouldn't call it help, exactly. They both worked and were busy. I'm not complaining—Mom usually made supper and didn't want rent or anything. And they never minded watching the babies while I made a diaper run."

He frowned, reading between the lines. "You were taking care of the babies by yourself."

"For the most part. I have to admit, I was nervous about moving here on my own, but it's been better than I'd hoped for. I hadn't realized seeing all my baking things would get me so excited. I've missed it. I can't wait to get started on your aunt's house."

Put like that, he could hardly lecture her.

He felt the same about ranching. Feeding the cattle, laughing at their antics, riding out all over his property made him feel alive.

"When we're done eating, take a look at the pictures and tell me if you think making the house is still feasible," he said.

"It will be." She took another bite. "What did you do today? What exactly is involved with ranching in December, anyhow?"

Flattered she'd asked, he almost launched into a full description of his winter ranch tasks, but he didn't want to bore her. "The most important thing is to feed the herd. We spread hay for them twice a day, and we measure it to see how much they're eating."

"What do you mean you measure it? Like weighing it?"

"Yes, and we measure the length of the feed line after we unroll it in the pasture. It gives us a chance to see how much the cows are wasting."

"Do they waste much?"

"Sometimes. With the ground frozen, less hay gets trampled into the dirt, though, so this weather helps. I don't like wasting hay."

"I know the feeling. I'm constantly checking the triplets' bottles to see how much they're eating. Amelia is my light eater, and I hate dumping formula down the drain." She took another bite.

"Does she worry you?"

"She did, but the doctor told me it's normal. She's just little." Nicole took a drink of water. "What else do you do out there? Do you ride horseback in this weather?"

"Not for feeding. I have a tractor that unrolls the hay bales for me. After that, yes, I saddle up and ride out as long as it's not icy. Got to protect my horses."

"Do you have calves right now?"

"No, we sold them last month. The cows are pregnant. We'll be calving late February through early April."

They continued talking about the triplets' schedule and his ranch work until Amelia whimpered. The boys were growing restless, too. Nicole had half a bowl of chili left, and he'd already finished seconds. He wanted her to be able to eat, but he didn't know what the babies needed.

She gave the boys their pacifiers, but Amelia didn't want hers and let out a cry.

Judd took his bowl into the kitchen and put it in the sink. "I'll hold her while you finish eating."

"You don't mind?"

"Why would I mind?" He took her out of the carrier, enjoying the weight of her small body in his arms. She sure was cute. He made faces at her until she smiled, and he sat back down across from Nicole. When she finished her chili, she reached behind her and grabbed the envelope, then shuffled through the pictures.

"Oh, these are perfect. The side views help. I'll be able to draw up the wall plans and create a paper model to make sure it all fits together."

"How do you do that?"

"I'll sketch the walls to scale, cut them out and tape them together. It will help give us a visual when we're assembling the real thing."

It sounded like a lot of work to him, but she seemed to think it would be fun. All he knew was Aunt Gretchen was going to love it.

"I appreciate you going to all this trouble to help me." He took in her shimmering eyes and sucked in a breath. His entire body warmed, and it wasn't from the chili.

Nicole was beautiful. Uncomplicated. Special.

"Are you in a hurry to leave?" She began clearing the table. "If not, I can sketch out a few of the walls so you can get an idea of what we'll be making."

He should leave. Shouldn't stay. This attraction was wrong on every level. "Go ahead."

"I was hoping you'd say that."

"Why don't I clear the table and do the dishes?" He stood and handed Nicole the baby. He'd stay a short while and then go home. "Then you can sketch all you want."

"You'd do that? Thanks." The gratitude

in her voice sent a fresh wave of shame to his gut. If she knew he wasn't offering out of the kindness of his heart, she'd be mortified. She thought of him as a friend. He'd have to do his best to hide his attraction.

Quickly, he cleared the table and loaded the dishwasher, tossed in a cleaning tab and wiped down the countertop. When he returned to the dining table, Nicole had Amelia tucked in one arm, and she was attempting to draw with her other hand.

"That will never work. Let me." He reached for the baby.

"I have to admit it is a lot easier to draw when I can actually hold the ruler and the paper."

He entertained Amelia for the next ten minutes until the boys got cranky.

"I need to change their diapers." She put the pencil down and stretched her neck from side to side.

"I'll help." Why had those words come out of his mouth? He didn't know the first thing about diapering. What if he did it wrong? What if something gross was in there? *Like you don't deal with manure every day on the ranch, you big wimp.*

She picked up each boy and carried them to the bedroom. He followed with Amelia. Nicole showed him where the diapers and wipes were after setting one of the babies in a crib while she changed the other.

"Do you want to try it?" she asked.

He didn't. And it wasn't because he was grossed out or anything. For some reason, he felt shy about the whole thing. It felt intimate. Too intimate.

"Just put her on the table..."

He placed Amelia on the changing table the way Nicole demonstrated. Getting the stretchy pants off almost gave him heartburn. What if he scratched her? Her legs were so tiny. But the baby simply grabbed her little feet and gurgled. The diaper was next. He tried not to look, just grabbed a wad of wipes and started dabbing.

"You only need one wipe, not half the container." Nicole pressed her lips together to keep from laughing.

"Sorry." Heat rushed up his neck. He kept Amelia from wiggling away as he tried to unfold a new diaper. How in the world did this woman do it with three babies? He couldn't even get one diapered, and he felt as if he'd been trying for two hours. Finally, he got the diaper under Amelia's bottom, and when Nicole told him to press the sticker tabs, he obeyed.

There. He'd changed a diaper.

He lifted Amelia and the diaper slid right off.

The baby made happy chirpy noises. At least one of them was enjoying this.

"Fasten the tabs a little tighter." Nicole had both boys in her arms again.

"Maybe you'd better do it."

"You've got this."

He sighed and, sticking his tongue out to the side, refastened the diaper. This time it stayed.

Beads of sweat had broken out on his forehead, and after he got Amelia's stretchy pants back on, he picked her up and discreetly wiped his forehead with the back of his hand.

"Good job. You're a pro now." Nicole's green eyes danced.

"I don't know about that," he said. "I'd better get out of your hair."

"Would you mind waiting a minute?" She led the way down the hall. "I have a list of ingredients I need, and I'm wondering if I should order everything or pick them up in town."

"Give me the list, and I'll buy it all." Back in the dining room, he set Amelia in her seat as Nicole got the boys settled.

"Most of it is standard stuff you'll find at the grocery store, but I don't have a base."

"A base?"

"Yes, a hard surface to build the gingerbread house on. That way we can move it easily."

He scratched his chin, trying to picture it. "What do you usually use?"

"We've used sturdy cardboard boxes or even nice wooden bases." She gestured to the living room. "I have plenty of boxes, but they're all too big. I need something less than an inch in height."

"I'll take care of it." He knew exactly who to talk to. Stu Miller. The rancher made custom cutting boards in his spare time. "Anything else?"

She disappeared into the kitchen for a moment and returned holding out a piece of paper. He scanned it, didn't see anything out of the ordinary, folded the paper and put it in his pocket.

"If I forgot anything, I'll let you know." She pushed up the sleeves of her sweater. "When do you want to get started?"

"I should be able to have the walls sketched out tomorrow night. Do you have plans on Saturday?"

"I do now. I have to get my ranch chores done in the morning, though."

"Then you can come out and play?" She grinned.

He wanted to tease her back, to joke the way she did so effortlessly, but he simply nodded.

After he put on his coat and boots, he paused in front of the door. "Thanks for the meal."

"You're welcome."

When he was halfway down the lane to his house, he realized his problem. She made him feel young again, like it was the most natural thing in the world for them to hang out and for her to tease him.

The cold air crept under his collar. Had he ever been young? Sometimes he thought he'd been born an old man.

If he'd had a friend like Nicole growing up, he might not be so awkward now. As it was, he was mature enough to know at this stage of his life, he wouldn't be content with only being friends. He just hoped she'd never catch on.

Because he needed her friendship. More than she could possibly understand.

# *Chapter Five*

Judd parked his truck in front of Stu Miller's stables and stepped onto the gravel drive Thursday afternoon. His breath blew in visible spirals, but he didn't feel cold. His sweatshirt, Carhartt jacket and jeans kept him plenty warm. Up ahead Dylan Kingsley pushed a wheelbarrow full of straw to the corral where Judd assumed they were keeping their steers. Dylan waved to him, calling, "Stu's in the stables."

"Thanks." He took a moment to gaze out over the spread. He'd always like Stu's ranch. It was orderly and old-school.

Nothing ostentatious, unlike his own huge house. Not that he was complaining; he loved his home, even if it was too big for one person. Black cattle in the distance broke up the white snow on the ground, and the blue sky didn't have a cloud in it.

"What can I do you for?" Stu strode out of the stables. He was wearing a thick plaid red-and-black jacket, jeans and cowboy boots. His gray hair matched his mustache. He was a tall man with a slight paunch. A toothpick bobbed between his teeth. Like Judd, he was a single rancher without any children. Unlike Judd, Stu was in his early seventies.

"You still doing woodwork on the side?" Judd joined him at the fence where a few horses seemed to be enjoying the brisk air.

"I am." Stu propped a boot on the lower rail of the fence and stared out at the horses.

"I'm working on a surprise for Aunt Gretchen. It's a Christmas gift."

"Gretchen, huh?" Stu turned to him, his face lighting up.

"Yeah, the plan is to bake her a gingerbread house styled after her childhood home."

Stu got a faraway look in his eye. "Is this the same one framed in her entryway?"

"That's the one." What was Stu doing at his aunt's house? Judd chided himself. The man had lived in this town forever, and Aunt Gretchen was known for her hospitality.

"She'll like that." Stu nodded, turning to face the pasture once more. "What do you need me to do? I ain't much of a baker."

Judd chuckled. "I'm not, either. Nicole Taylor—she's staying in one of my empty cabins with the triplets—she worked at a bakery." Saying the words made him uncomfortable. Would Stu read more into it?

"I know Nicole. Remember seeing her in town as a young 'un with her ma and sister. They were a cute bunch. I remember when that fella of hers found out he had a disease in high school. She stuck with him, married him, too. Not many gals would do that, you know."

He did know, and it wasn't helping him feel any better about the situation.

"Doesn't seem fair, does it?" Stu's toothpick went up. "Having to raise three babies by herself. Makes me wonder." He shook his head.

What? What did it make him wonder?

"And now her ma up and moved away with her boyfriend… Gretchen and Lois told me about it. I'm glad you gave Nicole a home. You're a fine man, Judd."

His neck grew hot. He didn't know what to say. He wasn't the great guy Stu was making him out to be. It wasn't as if he could make Stu understand, either. *She's cooking me dinner each night* sounded weird.

"I take it you're looking for me to make something for this gingerbread house."

"Uh, yes." Judd was grateful for the change in subject. "I need a wooden base. Less than an inch thick. Nothing too heavy. I have the dimensions here." He pulled out a folded paper from his back pocket and handed it to Stu. "Think you could do it? We'd need it pretty quickly."

"Can I do it?" He acted like Judd had made a joke. "Of course I can do it. If it makes your aunt happy, I'm glad to help. I'll have it to you tomorrow night."

"You don't have to drop everything on my account."

Stu laughed. "What do I have to drop? I'm an old man. It'll give me something to do."

The way he said it made Judd frown. He had a lot in common with the rancher. No wife, no kids, just a large cattle ranch and a herd that depended on him. Was this what his future would look like? Unlike Stu, he didn't even have a hobby.

Judd thought about his estate planning and how he'd gotten nowhere with it.

"Stu, do you mind if I ask for a bit of advice?"

"Shoot."

"I'm making some long-term plans, and I'm kind of stuck."

"No heir." He nodded, leaning against the top fence rail. "I've been there."

If he'd been there, that must mean he wasn't there any longer. It gave Judd hope. "What did you do?"

"I didn't think about it much when I was a young buck, but I guess I was about your age when it started bothering me."

Good, maybe what he was going through was normal.

"It was about that time I started relying on Josiah more and more. I knew he respected the ranch the way I did, so I named him in my will. After he died last year, I had to rethink things. Then Dylan came along, and...problem solved." Stu's toothpick bobbed up and down.

Disappointment dripped down to his boots. He'd been hoping Stu would have the perfect solution for him.

"Who's your right-hand man, Judd?"

"I couldn't say for sure." He liked both of his ranch hands, Dallas and Clay, but he didn't exactly have a right-hand man. While he knew they liked working for him, he doubted they loved the ranch the way he did. It didn't seem to be in their blood the way it was in his.

Stu studied him, and Judd fought the urge to squirm.

"You could take the normal route. Get married. Have kids."

Judd didn't bother suppressing his grimace. He wasn't exactly normal.

"Don't look so green, son. There's a quality gal staying in a cabin down the lane from you. She's got her hands full, sure, but she'd make a good wife."

"Her husband hasn't been dead a year." The words came out with more force than he intended.

"Yep, and time's a tickin'."

"I didn't mean it like that."

"I know you didn't. I'm teasing you." Stu wagged his finger toward Judd's face. "A marriage is a good place to start when you're estate planning."

"I'm not getting married just to name someone in my will."

"That would be foolish. I agree. But if

a special someone were to come along, you'd best rent a tux and get to the church."

"I've never rented a tux in my life." He regretted the words the instant they came out.

"There's a first time for everything, son." Stu clapped his hand on Judd's shoulder. "Come on. Let's pick out the wood for Gretchen's present."

Judd followed him to a pole barn. There had to be a better way to plan his estate than to get married. He didn't want to spend the rest of his life on pins and needles waiting for his bride to get fed up with him and leave. If his previous relationships were any indication, that was exactly what he had to look forward to.

Naming Dallas or Clay in his will might be his best option.

Early Saturday afternoon, Nicole carefully arranged her long hair into a messy, but not *too* messy, bun on top of her head. She'd actually put on makeup as well. With a few pumps of hair spray and a quick swipe of raspberry-colored lip gloss, she deemed herself ready.

*Ready for what?*

Judd's handsome face danced through her mind.

*Baking. I'm ready for the baking.*

On her way to the living room, she paused in front of the babies' room—she'd put them down for a nap a few minutes ago—and hearing nothing, she continued forward. Thursday night Judd had dropped off all the ingredients on her list. And yesterday morning, Jane Boyd had shown up in full grandmother mode. Jane was a former church choir director, who could probably handle six babies at once. The woman had taken charge and shooed Nicole out of the way.

Exactly what she'd needed. She'd been thrilled to find out Jane would be coming every Friday. As the woman sang to the babies in their bouncy seats, Nicole had used the time to whip up a few batches of gingerbread dough to chill. And last night she'd finished cutting out the wall templates and taped them together to make a model of the house. She couldn't wait to show it to Judd.

Checking the time, she frowned. The triplets would be napping for two hours. It wouldn't be enough time to roll out and bake all of the walls. She'd need to make more dough at some point in there, too, because the house was going to be on the large side, the size of a small dollhouse.

A few taps on the door sent her pulse racing. She practically tripped over her own feet on her way to open it. Judd stood there, his Carhartt unzipped, a navy Henley hugging his abs, cowboy hat tilted just so on his dark hair. His lips curved up, and her heartbeat thumped in her chest.

Who knew a cowboy could look so good?

"Come in." She waved him inside. She didn't notice the piece of wood he'd tucked under his arm until he set it on the floor against the wall. "Is that the base?"

"Yes. Stu Miller made it for me. It's nice, isn't it?"

"Wow, he's talented." She picked it up and admired the smooth stained piece he'd made alternating two types of wood. "He did this so quickly, too."

As Judd shimmied out of his jacket, she averted her eyes. Those broad shoulders were not to be looked at or temptation might strike. Checking out the man who'd generously blessed her with this cabin would be inappropriate. Not to mention it would be embarrassing if he caught her. Instead, she strode to the dining table, where she'd constructed the paper house. Judd joined her.

"You did all this?" He let out a low whistle. "You could have been an architect. It looks exactly like the picture. And you labeled them all, too."

She tried not to let his compliment go to her head, but she was pretty sure her heart was lit up like the Christmas tree in downtown Rendezvous. "The labels help with construction. I made some dough last night so we could start baking right away."

"What should I do?" He rubbed his hands together.

"Why don't you take apart the paper walls and bring them to me. I'll start rolling out the dough so we can cut them out." She went into the kitchen and turned on the oven to preheat it.

"Got it." He took one step then paused. "What do you say we put on some Christmas music?"

Christmas music? Her stomach lurched. She'd been avoiding it as much as possible, afraid a chorus of festive music would bring back the nightmare she'd gone through last year.

Aaron's persistent cough. The misdiagnosis. The tests. Then the ICU. Holding his hand night and day as he'd fought for his life.

The endless tears she'd cried.

The panic in her soul.

Not being able to eat. Worrying not only for her husband, but also for the precious three lives in her womb. Pleading with God in the hospital chapel.

What if a few bars of "Holly Jolly Christmas" threw her right back into the black place she'd been last December?

"Nicole?" Concern flickered through Judd's eyes.

She forgot to breathe, forgot where she was momentarily. She shook her head. "I don't want to wake the triplets."

Great, now she was a liar, too.

"Actually, it's not that." She stared down at her feet, having no words to explain and not wanting to if she had them. "Go ahead. Put the music on."

She pivoted, made a beeline for the sheet pans and started tearing off parchment paper to line them. If the memories came and she fell apart… No. She was stronger now, better than she'd been last year. She'd be fine. The dough would distract her. Where was the supersharp knife she always used for cutting out the walls?

Her nerves were ping-ponging around like popcorn popping. So what? It didn't mean she was on the verge of a nervous breakdown.

"We don't have to have music."

She almost jumped. Judd had followed her into the kitchen.

"It's okay. Really." She attempted a smile but the dread in her gut overrode it. "'Tis the season, right?"

"Don't you like Christmas?" He leaned against the counter, watching her with a thoughtful expression.

"I do. Everyone likes Christmas." Her shrill tone made her cringe.

"You don't have to pretend with me, Nicole." He was right. She didn't have to pretend with him. Out of everyone in Rendezvous, he had not once pressured her to talk about her feelings or open up about her grief or any of the other things her well-meaning friends had urged her to do.

"It's..." She didn't know how to put it into words. "I can't explain it."

"You don't have to." The kindness in his eyes brought a different kind of ache to her heart. "We'll skip the music."

And that was why she never should have

volunteered to make this gingerbread house with Judd Wilson.

He got her in a way no one else did.

Not trusting herself to speak, she nodded and picked up her rolling pin. Then she took out an oval of dough and began rolling it out onto a sheet of parchment paper. After measuring it for the precise thickness—all the walls needed to be uniform—she stood back and eyed it.

"Do you have any of the paper walls untaped?" she asked.

"I'll bring them over." He'd stacked them as he'd separated them. His hand brushed hers as he passed them to her. The hair on her arms rose at his touch, and the smell of his skin was a melding of pine and spice and fresh air.

The kitchen seemed to shrink, and all she could hear was the faint sound of the furnace kicking on. Well, that and her thumping heartbeat.

She hadn't felt this jumpy since she'd downed three energy drinks and feared she was having a stroke the week she'd started at the bakery.

If pure silence only magnified Judd's presence here, maybe she'd be better off with the Christmas tunes. It would remind her of Aaron. Then she wouldn't do anything stupid. Like get too close to Judd.

"On second thought, why don't you play some Christmas music. I have a small speaker you can link your phone to." She waved in the direction of the living room. "It's next to the television."

"Are you sure? I'll keep the volume low."

She nodded, not sure at all. Leafing through the templates, she selected the ones that would fit on the rolled-out dough. Then she cut them out, put the excess dough on a piece of wax paper, pricked the walls and slid them onto a half-sheet pan. After sliding it into the oven, she set the timer and grabbed another batch from the fridge.

An instrumental version of "Greensleeves" floated through the speaker, and she froze.

Memories of last year barreled in. The smells and beeps and harsh lights in the hospital she'd tucked away all rushed back. The raw fear, the pleading prayers, the terror of losing the man who had been her rock for most of her life was still there. Still a part of her.

It would always be a part of her.

No matter what the rest of her life held, the years with Aaron would never be erased. She didn't want them to be, even though his final weeks had brought so much sadness.

Bracing her hands against the counter, she closed her eyes and willed the tightness in her throat to subside. She sensed Judd behind her and, turning, slowly opened her eyes.

The man was solid. Real. Healthy. Understanding. And he stood there with an air of *you can lean on me*, so she did. She stepped closer and wrapped her arms around his waist, letting her cheek rest against his chest. The softness of his shirt, the warmth of his body and the steady beat of his heart comforted her. And then his arms slipped behind her back, holding her gently as if she might break.

She couldn't break, though.

She'd already been broken.

As the seconds stretched to a minute, she couldn't help wishing he'd hold her forever.

Forever?

She snapped back to reality and pulled away, keeping her gaze down. No man had held her except Aaron. Shouldn't she hate the sensation? Fight it? Or, at the very least, be uncomfortable?

She certainly shouldn't like it as much as she did.

"I'm sorry." Nicole took a few more steps backward, touching the back of her hair as she shook her head. What could she say? She didn't want him to know how much she liked being in his arms. "I've been avoiding reminders of last year."

"I should have realized..."

"No, you didn't know. I guess I didn't

want to get sucked into the bad memories from Christmas."

"But you did get sucked in, didn't you? I'll turn off the music. In fact, I can leave. This isn't a good time." He moved away.

"Wait—you can keep it on." She didn't want him to leave. This was gingerbread day. She'd been looking forward to it all week. The last thing she wanted to do was dwell on where she was at a year ago. "I can't exactly avoid Christmas forever, you know. And this *is* a good time. I'll roll out these walls, and you can cut them out, okay?"

His eyes searched hers, and she was certain he could see all the way to the very memories she feared. Finally, he nodded. "I'll finish taking the tape off the walls."

She picked up the rolling pin and tried to get a grip on her emotions. Smoothing out the dough calmed her nerves, and when "Holly Jolly Christmas" came on, an older memory came back of her ice-skating with Stella when they were kids.

Not every memory was bad. Not all Christmas songs led back to Aaron.

"Are you ready to cut?" She motioned for Judd to join her.

Maybe getting through this Christmas wasn't about avoiding the past, but making peace with it.

"This doesn't look right." Judd tried to fit the final two paper walls on the sheet of dough Nicole rolled out, but they kept overlapping. They'd been baking for hours and taking plenty of breaks to care for the triplets, who were lined up in bouncy seats nearby.

Nicole had been quiet after he'd held her but, after a while, she'd begun to open up. She told him about growing up without a dad, and how she and her mom didn't always see eye to eye. She also shared how she and Aaron had become inseparable in elementary school, and how she'd relied on him throughout her life. Judd even found himself thankful she'd had Aaron, which surprised him. He himself could never live up to the guy, but he was glad Nicole had been blessed with a good husband. She deserved it.

He, in turn, told her how he'd grown up in the city but never felt at home there. He hadn't talked much about his parents, though. He and Nicole had shared a few laughs about his attempts at playing soccer in third grade. Kicking a ball down a field had never made much sense to him.

An hour ago, he'd held Henry and fed him his bottle while Nicole fed the other two. Of course, she'd told Judd he didn't have to, but he'd wanted to. Today was turning out to be one of the best days he'd had in ages.

From behind him, Nicole peered over his shoulder. He turned to see what she wanted. The stray hairs from her bun curled around her face, tempting him to push them back behind her ear. She pointed to the dough. "If you turn this one, they should both fit."

"Oh." He flipped it around. "You're right."

"Of course I'm right." Her toothy grin

had him shaking his head. He couldn't remember ever feeling this relaxed with a woman before.

He still felt guilty about the Christmas music earlier. It hadn't occurred to him hearing it would make her sad. He should have picked up on her cues. But holding her, comforting her after? He'd probably regret it at some point, but right now he didn't.

Having her in his arms had felt right—more than right. Like sitting before a crackling fire after a long day out in the cold. Or watching a herd of wild horses running free on the farthest borders of his land. Not a lot touched his soul, but having Nicole in his arms sure had.

"Are your parents still alive, Judd?"

"Yes."

"Tell me about them."

His parents? He'd rather not. He finished cutting out the pieces and pierced the dough the way she'd shown him. "There's not much to tell."

"Give me the short version." She checked

the batch baking in the oven and closed the oven door. "We've got another ten minutes before this needs to come out. Let's sit in the living room."

Together, they moved the babies to the living room.

"They could use a little tummy time." Nicole placed Amelia, stomach down, on a quilted mat, then laid Henry next to her. When she added Eli to the group, the boy cried loud and hard.

"I'll take him." Judd gestured for her to hand him the baby. He kept Eli on his lap and watched Nicole praise Amelia and Henry for craning their necks and attempting to shift positions.

Judd had been awestruck watching her juggle the babies and bake all day. If the children fussed, she moved them to bouncy seats or played with them on the floor for a few minutes. Her phone alarm alerted her to feeding times and nap times. When they all got cranky, she calmly attended to each one until they stopped crying.

She was amazing.

"I take it you don't have any siblings?" With a burp cloth, Nicole wiped the drool spilling from Amelia's mouth onto the mat.

"No," he said. "Just me."

"Parents—together or divorced?"

"Together, still living near Boston. For the moment, anyhow. They bought a condo in Saint Thomas."

"Oh, a warm island sounds so good right now. Have you gone down there? If your parents have a condo, it's like your own vacation spot, right?" She made cute faces at Henry, who grunted and stretched his legs as he tried to roll to his side.

"I'm afraid not. They purchased it recently." Normally, he'd downplay or not discuss his parents, but Nicole hadn't held back telling him her feelings about her mom. He figured he owed her the same candor. "I called them the other night. I was going to visit them after Christmas, and that's when Mom told me they'd bought the condo. They're probably on their way down to Saint Thomas now."

"I'm sorry." Her lips turned down in sympathy. "Looks like we're both on our own for Christmas this year."

"I'm used to it. I always spend Christmas with Aunt Gretchen. My parents are too busy to get together with me." He hoped he didn't sound bitter. "I sometimes wonder if the nurses switched me with their real son at birth. I couldn't be more opposite from them."

"What do you mean?"

"They spend most nights socializing. I prefer to be alone."

She chuckled. "I understand. My mom and sister are a lot alike, too. Their top priority is having a man in their life. I guess I shouldn't talk. I always had Aaron."

Henry made spitting noises with his tongue. And then he rolled onto his back.

"Did you see that?" Nicole rose on her knees, pointing to Henry. "He rolled over!"

She scooped up the baby and rained kisses on both cheeks before planting one on his tummy. The boy squealed with delight.

"He's strong, isn't he?" Judd couldn't drag his gaze away from Nicole's sparkling eyes and the way she loved on Henry. Eli, meanwhile, began to get cranky. Judd tried to make the baby comfortable.

"Yes, a lot of babies roll over even earlier, but I haven't been worried." She set Henry back down on the quilt as Eli squawked.

"Oh, Eli, I didn't forget about you. No need to be jealous." She took him from Judd to lay him down on his stomach with his siblings. He fussed a little bit, and Nicole set a small stuffed cat within his reach. "You wait. He'll be rolling over in the next day or two."

"What about Amelia?" Would she be as strong as her brothers?

"She's been trying." Nicole moved to sit on the couch since the babies were occupied. She continued to keep a watchful eye on them. "How did you end up with the ranch?"

"My uncle Gus. I moved out here at eighteen. He taught me the ins and outs of ranching, and between him and Aunt Gretchen, I was pretty blessed."

"Remind me again—was Gretchen his wife?"

"No, his sister. My dad is their younger brother." From the corner of his eye, he noticed Amelia pushing herself up on her arms. He held his breath a moment, but she dropped back to her original position.

"Gus never married?"

"No. No kids, either. I inherited the ranch from him. And now I find myself in a similar situation."

"What do you mean?" She pulled her knee to her chest, cocking her head to the side. "No wife or kids?"

"No heir." He opened his hands. "Makes estate planning difficult."

"Are you worried about dying?" She half-heartedly chuckled. "You're not ill or anything, are you?"

"No, of course not. I'm just getting older and want to be prepared."

She nodded thoughtfully. "Have you talked to Mason Fanning? I know he struggled after his first wife died. He might have some advice."

"I didn't think of him." Judd highly doubted Mason had worried about who to leave his ranch to, since he'd had a son before his wife died, but he might as well talk to Mason. It wasn't as if he had anything to lose at this point.

Amelia pushed herself up again. "I think she wants to prove something to her brothers." He pointed to the girl. She tipped to the side. He caught Nicole's gaze and they both turned to watch as Amelia toppled onto her back.

"Two in one day!" Nicole went to Amelia and proceeded to kiss her again and again.

The oven timer went off.

"You stay there." Judd rose. "It's way past supper time. I'm not much of a cook, but I can make grilled cheese sandwiches for us."

"I know I should object, but grilled

cheese sounds amazing." She held Amelia high in the air, and the baby let out a hearty laugh.

"Relax. I'll take care of everything."

It was a day of firsts for the babies. And for him. For the first time in his life, he wanted to stay right here and keep talking to a woman. Not just any woman. This woman.

And it didn't scare him.

But maybe it should.

What a day of contrasts. Nicole pulled a soft throw over her legs. She'd put the babies to bed, changed into her pajamas and turned on the cooking channel. Judd had left over an hour ago, promising he'd drive her and the triplets to church in the morning. Having an extra pair of hands for the process of getting to and from church would be welcome.

Earlier, Judd's presence had kept her from lingering in the dark places the Christmas music had taken her to. He'd helped with the babies as well. If he hadn't been here, there was no way she'd have been able to bake the walls.

From low to high. Sadness to sheer happiness. Yes, she'd come close to falling apart at memories of Aaron's death, but leaning on Judd, baking and watching her babies roll over had brought her joy.

Now she was going to lose herself in a holiday cooking competition and not think about Aaron or Christmas or the cowboy who was so patient with her babies and with her.

Nicole's cell phone rang. Maybe it was Judd. She shot to a seated position and grabbed her phone. A flush of anticipation spread through her. The anticipation vanished when she saw her mother-in-law's name on the screen. "Hello?"

"I hope this is a good time," Sherry said.

"Perfect timing. The babies are asleep."

"Oh, good." Sherry sounded relieved. "How are you holding up?"

Nicole always felt awkward when Aaron's mom asked that question, and she asked it every time she called. "Pretty good. I'm getting close to being unpacked."

"I'm glad. It sounds as if your friends came through for you with all their help. Lance and I are thankful."

"I am, too." Her mother-in-law had always been thoughtful.

"The holiday season hasn't been easy for us, and we figured it's been probably ten times worse for you. It's hard to believe Aaron's gone. It's even harder to believe it's been a year already."

"Almost." Nicole thought of all the Sunday dinners she'd eaten with the Taylors here in Rendezvous before they all moved away. But she and Aaron hadn't lived near any family in over five years, and she wasn't as close to them anymore. "The babies help keep my mind off things."

"It helps us, too, being involved with the grandchildren. They bring so much life back to the house."

Sherry and Lance spent a lot of time with their other grandchildren on account of living within two miles of both Aaron's sisters.

"How are the kiddos doing? Is Jaycee recovered?" Aaron's sisters, Jaycee and Alyssa, were older than her and had each other, so Nicole had never been very close to them. She liked them both just the same.

"It's still touch and go. The doctor said she might need surgery. Her knee isn't healing on its own."

"Tell her I'm sorry she's going through this. It can't be easy with the baby and a toddler."

"I will." Sherry hesitated. "You know, you and the triplets have been on our minds and in our prayers a lot lately. We were surprised—shocked, really—when you told us your mom moved to Florida on such short notice. We're concerned about you."

"I know—it was a shock to me, too. But I'm holding up well. Some of the ladies from church take turns coming in weekday mornings to help me out. They've been such a blessing. And my friends babysit for me when I need to get groceries."

"We're glad you have help." Her voice sounded strained. "Lance and I would like to come visit you and the triplets for a few days before Christmas. We'll book a room at the inn in town. Would that be all right with you?"

"Of course." She hoped they wouldn't judge her parenting skills. Not that they would. They'd never been the overly judgy type. She was just being sensitive. Triplets were more than a handful, and she was doing the best she could. "Do you have dates in mind?"

"We'll fly in on Friday, December 18 and leave that Sunday. We plan on catching up with some of our friends while we're in town, too."

"I'm looking forward to it. You won't believe how much the babies have grown." The last time they'd visited had been a month after the children were born. Nicole's energy had been nonexistent and she'd barely been able to keep up with round-the-clock feedings and no sleep. What a difference a few months made.

"They are the most adorable little ones. Thank you for sending us pictures so often. We appreciate it."

"I love showing them off. By the way, Henry rolled over for the first time today. And Amelia followed..." They chitchatted about the triplets and life in general for a while.

After hanging up, Nicole set the phone on the end table and lay back on the couch, pulling the throw up to her chin.

For the past year her life had moved in a new direction. She'd been raising the babies as best as she knew how. In some ways, Sherry and Lance coming to visit felt like her old life and new life were colliding.

Maybe the problem was that she'd defined herself by Aaron most of her life. And now that he was gone? Well, the past months had been liberating in a sense. She'd been able to accept her new role as a single mom. She no longer spent her days mourning for her husband.

Would her in-laws be offended? Think less of her?

How did one navigate extended family in a time like this?

She wasn't sure, but the nagging sensation inside her chest told her to tread carefully.

# Chapter Six

People were talking about him and Nicole.

Judd might not have a way with words, but he had a knack for sizing up the unspoken things so easy to miss. For the fifteenth time since the church service began, he squirmed in the back pew of the church.

He'd driven Nicole and the babies in her minivan this morning. The ride had been uneventful. She told him her in-laws were coming in a few weeks and that her friends were stopping by this afternoon. He shared with her the long list of things he needed to check on the ranch before the snow started coming down tonight.

Judd was used to sitting toward the front of the church on the right-hand side with Aunt Gretchen. When he'd helped carry the babies in, Nicole told him she always sat in the back. Not wanting to leave her alone, he'd stayed by her side, but then Gabby, Dylan and little Phoebe had joined them, and at that point Judd felt out of place. He'd considered excusing himself to sit with Aunt Gretchen, but Stu Miller had slid in next to her.

It had unsettled him, seeing Stu in his spot.

That was when Judd began noticing the discreet glances of the congregation. They sneaked peeks at him sitting with Nicole. Never mind there was a baby carrier separating them. He could tell Rendezvous would be abuzz with speculation in no time flat.

A worship song played—one of the new contemporary ones he actually liked—and he sang along, keeping an eye on Henry, who was staring up at him from the car seat to his left. To his right was Eli's car seat. Nicole sat between Eli's and Amelia's. Gabby had taken Amelia out of the carrier and was holding her, while Dylan held her one-year-old, Phoebe.

After the song ended, the pastor read from the Bible, but Judd didn't hear a word. Henry looked like he was getting antsy. Should he take him out? Nicole was too far away to do it. He couldn't exactly ask her with Eli between them. Henry grunted, then squawked, and his little face grew red.

Judd unstrapped him and lifted him out of the car seat. The boy's lips jutted out, but he didn't make a peep. In fact, his normal color returned. Then he smiled at Judd.

His heart was doing funny things, like when his favorite horse, Candy, pranced during a gentle snow with the big flakes coming down. Watching the baby smile gave him the same happy feeling.

"Thank you," Nicole whispered. Her

green eyes shimmered with appreciation, and he nodded to her, ignoring the way his pulse reacted. The baby liked him, and Nicole needed help, and…now he was glad he was the one sitting back here helping her.

He settled Henry on his lap for the rest of the service. The child let out a sigh of contentment and sank into his arms. At some point, Nicole took Eli out and held him. He let out a few noises during the sermon, but she held him to her shoulder and patted his back to soothe him.

When church ended, Judd strapped Henry back in his seat and helped Nicole get all the car seats locked onto the stroller frame. He followed her to the large entryway and wasn't surprised when several older women, along with Nicole's girlfriends, surrounded her. He hung back.

"It's awfully nice of you to help her out." Lois Dern, his aunt's best friend, came up and gave him a hug. He was used to her hugs and had to bend down to return it.

She had short white hair and always told it like it was but with a grin.

"Thanks, Lois, but I'm not doing much."

Her eyes twinkled as if to say *you don't fool me*. "I had to get up during the sermon, and I saw you holding the baby. He looked good in your arms. You've got the touch."

"Just habit. I'm used to dealing with calves."

"Calves are not the same as babies." She rolled her eyes and waved him off. "Is there a romantic bone in your body?"

Romance? The hair on the back of his neck rose. Why would he need a romantic bone in his body? He was just helping out a friend.

"I'm afraid there isn't, Lois." He shrugged. "Nicole needed a ride and an extra set of hands with the babies. That's it."

"If you say so."

"It's thoughtful of you and Aunt Gretch and the other ladies to be helping her out during the week." Movement by the coatracks caught his eye. Stu was helping his aunt get her coat on.

"I'm in all my glory. I can't get enough of those babies. It's been too long since I held an infant. And Nicole is a good little mama, let me tell you. They'll be raised right. The only thing missing is for them to have a daddy."

He tried not to react to her comment. Was she hinting that he should be their daddy? He ran a finger under his collar.

"Don't get all scared. I was just making an observation."

Aunt Gretchen and Stu came over and joined them. They discussed the upcoming bake sale for Christmas Fest. Judd looked around for Nicole. She was talking to Gabby, Eden and Brittany.

"I have a wonderful idea." Lois clapped her hands, turning to Aunt Gretchen. "Why don't we babysit the triplets Saturday afternoon after our shift at the church bake sale? Then Judd can take Nicole to Christmas Fest."

"Oh, yes, lovely idea." Aunt Gretchen's

entire face lit up with hope. "We'll be done by one, and you can get Nicole out and about, poor thing." She made a clucking sound. "But, Lois, do you think we can handle all three babies by ourselves?"

"I'll help out, too, ladies." With his hands in his pockets, Stu rocked back on his heels. His ever-present toothpick was nowhere to be seen. Judd peered closely, making sure he hadn't missed it. He rarely saw Stu without one.

"You?" Lois sounded incredulous. "I didn't know you had it in you, Stu. You're up for helping with tiny babies?"

"Sure, why not? I like kids. Never had any myself, but I bounced a babe on my knee a time or two." Stu sent a furtive sideways glance Aunt Gretchen's way.

"Well, these babies aren't old enough to be bounced, Stuart." His aunt's eyes grew round in seriousness. "We have to be very careful with them or they could get… Oh, what's that thing where shaking can hurt them, Lois?"

"Shaken baby syndrome, and I don't

think Stu is in any danger of bouncing them like that, anyhow. I'll see if Frank wants to join us. He's always had a soft spot for children." Lois pointed to Stu. "Meet us at Nicole's at 1:30 sharp on Saturday."

"Wait, wait." Judd held up his hands. "Doesn't Nicole have some say in this?"

He had to admit the thought of taking Nicole to Christmas Fest and ice-skating, buying hot chocolates, walking around the decorated town appealed to him a lot, but…

"Don't I have some say in what?" Nicole's smile spread from ear to ear, and the slight flush of her cheeks made her glow. She pushed the stroller next to him, and he forced his gaze from her face to check on the babies, who all appeared to be fine.

"Oh, good! Gretchen and I and Stu here want to babysit next Saturday afternoon so you can go to Christmas Fest. Judd will take you."

"I forgot about Christmas Fest." Nicole looked upward, a dreamy look in her eyes.

"Do they still have the outdoor skating rink?"

"Yes, if the weather cooperates." Aunt Gretchen nodded.

"And the reindeer? What about the crafts booths and the bake sale? I always loved going to it when I was a kid."

"All of that and more, honey." Lois skirted Stu and Gretchen to put her arm around Nicole. "We're manning the bake sale booth in the morning, but we'll come over right after. Then Judd will take you to the festival."

He opened his mouth to decline. People were already starting to talk. It wouldn't be appropriate for him to take her around town without the babies. What if everyone assumed it was a date?

His neck felt scratchy. Was he getting hives?

"You really wouldn't mind?" Nicole sounded so grateful. He turned his attention back to her, but she was talking to his aunt and Lois.

"Of course not. We're enjoying your babies. It's a treat for us to hold and feed and play with them." Aunt Gretchen patted her arm. "You'll see. Someday they'll be grown and you'll miss those babies in your arms."

"Well, I'd love that." She rested her chin on the tips of her steepled fingers. "I'll bake cupcakes for the bake sale, too."

"Don't knock yourself out," Lois said. "We know you've got your hands full."

"I love to bake. It's..." She averted her gaze momentarily. "Therapeutic."

Lois and Aunt Gretchen exchanged glances.

"Then we'd appreciate any baked goods you'd like to donate." Lois put her arm around Nicole's shoulders.

"Be ready at 1:30, Judd," Aunt Gretchen said.

"Oh..." Nicole bit her bottom lip. "I didn't even ask you what you wanted, Judd. You don't have to take me."

"He wants to take you." Aunt Gretchen patted Nicole's arm. "Don't you, Judd?"

He did.

And he shouldn't.

Yes, he'd enjoy spending the afternoon with Nicole. He usually avoided Christmas Fest, but it actually sounded like a good time. However, he didn't want her to have to deal with town gossip—especially not when it involved him.

He glanced at Nicole, and the hope on her face overrode his reluctance. "I'll take you."

"See?" Aunt Gretchen said. Lois, Aunt Gretchen and even Stu beamed.

An afternoon alone with Nicole at a heavily populated town event was not going to stop people's tongues from wagging. The last thing he wanted was for people to assume they were dating. They'd think he was too old for her—and they'd be right—or that something was going on at the ranch that shouldn't be. She didn't need any more troubles in her life. He had a feeling this Christmas was going to be hard enough on her as it was.

"You seem happier lately." Eden followed Nicole into her kitchen that afternoon. Gabby, Brittany and Mason had stopped by the cabin with a few Christmas decorations, and they'd strung garland and multicolored lights across the fireplace mantel for her. Then they'd added several snowmen and candles. It was night and day from the decorations Aaron had bought, and Nicole was glad. The room felt cozy. She'd gotten a little choked up at their thoughtfulness, but their banter had lightened the mood.

"I am happier." Nicole began warming up three bottles. "I think it's this cabin. Having my own space has been freeing."

"I know what you mean," Eden said. "I was so worried about moving off my parents' ranch and into my own apartment. At first, it was hard. But after a while, I started to like being independent."

Independent. Could Nicole say the same about herself? Not really. She was relying on the kindness of others for this cabin, for help with the babies and even for the opportunity to grocery shop by herself.

"That's great." Nicole closed the distance between them and hugged her. "You've been such a good friend to me. I want to see you happy."

Her expression fell. "I'm starting to think what I really want out of life isn't going to happen. Maybe I need to make peace with it."

"What do you mean?" She leaned against the counter and gave Eden her full attention.

"Oh, you know, the husband, kids, minivan and house." She let out a sad laugh. "I think I need to figure out how to be content with what I have."

"It's hard." Nicole weighed how honest she should be. "My whole life I thought I wanted one thing. To be Aaron's wife. Then it expanded to the kids, minivan and house."

"I'm sorry. I didn't mean to bring up... Just forget I said anything." Eden's cheeks grew pink.

"No, that's not why I'm telling you this." How could she explain? "I relied on Aaron for too much. We were both young when we got married. And as we matured, we didn't always want the same things. I loved him. He loved me. But I was always terrified of losing him, and part of the fear was love, yes, but a lot of it was the fear of being on my own. I didn't think I could handle life by myself."

Eden wore a thoughtful expression. "You know, this is the first time you've opened up about Aaron beyond his illness and death."

Nicole stared at her hands. It was true. She'd been in the role of the grieving widow for a long time. "I guess I don't need everyone feeling sorry for me anymore."

"We'll always sympathize with you."

"I know. But I'm ready to move past it. Our marriage wasn't a fairy tale, and sometimes I feel like people assume Aaron was Mr. Perfect because he died. Or they think I'm this superwoman taking care of three babies. He wasn't perfect, and I'm not, either. I'm tired of his death defining me. We had some shaky spots in our marriage. I trust you and the rest of our group enough to know you won't judge me for feeling this way."

"Believe it or not, I can relate to that." Eden tapped her finger against her chin. "For a long time after my sister, Mia, died, I couldn't bear to say anything negative about her to anyone. But as time wore on, I could admit to myself our relationship wasn't perfect. I think I needed to accept that when she died, our relationship would never get to the place I'd always hoped it would. It was hard to give her up, but it was also hard to give up the dreams I had for our future."

"What did your dreams look like?"

A small smile played on her lips. "I envisioned Christmases at my family's ranch where we'd sit around a tall Christmas tree with our kids and bake cookies and sip cocoa and watch movies on television. I figured we'd grow closer as we got older."

The image touched Nicole. She'd always wanted something similar. "I'm sorry you'll never have that with Mia."

"I am, too. And I'm sorry you won't have Aaron to grow old with."

Nicole tried to picture this Christmas if Aaron hadn't passed away. They'd be buying gifts for the triplets, decorating with the ugly blue and silver bulbs he'd bought, and she really wouldn't have minded them because the only thing that mattered was being with her loved ones.

*Lord, since You brought Aaron home to be with You, I've had to adjust my dreams. I know he's in paradise. It's hard to be the one left behind. But You've blessed me even through the tears and pain. It's strange, but I don't miss my old life with the same intensity I used to.*

"Maybe you don't have to give up on the entire dream, Eden."

"What do you mean?"

"You can still have some of those things—the husband and kids around the Christmas tree and the laughter and hot cocoa."

Eden gave her head a small, sad shake. "Mom and Dad are selling the ranch.

Mia's gone. I haven't had a date in—" she ticked off her fingers "—years and years. I don't see it happening."

"If you'd told me at this time last year that I'd be a widow with triplet babies and living back in Rendezvous, I would have been so terrified, I would have started vomiting and never stopped." She handed Eden a bottle and took the other two. "But God has given me peace, and I don't understand how or why, but most of the time, I'm okay."

"He doesn't give as the world gives." Eden wrapped her arm around Nicole's shoulders and gave her a little squeeze. "Thanks, Nicole."

"If you look at what you want, it boils down to love and connection. There's a guy out there who is going to love you so fiercely it will take your breath away. And, as for the connection, you'll always miss Mia, but you've got a roomful of friends who are always up for hot cocoa and laughter."

"You're right." Eden smiled. "When I think about what I have, it helps me be content."

Nicole gestured for Eden to follow her back to the living room. Mason came up to them, and Eden joined Gabby and Brittany and the babies.

"I'm going to talk to Judd for a while. Are you doing okay?" Mason was tall with dark blond hair, a lean frame and a heart of gold. He had an identical twin, Ryder, who lived in Los Angeles. Together they equaled two times the gorgeous. Nicole considered Mason a good friend.

"Moving in to this cabin has helped. I'm so thankful to have my own place."

"I'm glad. If you need to talk, I'm here. The first Christmas after Mia died was rough. And with Noah being a baby at the time, well, I was pretty exhausted. I spent more time riding out on my ranch than I probably should have. Trying to keeping busy. Avoiding my thoughts. I just wanted you to know we're all praying for you."

"Thanks, Mason." Was she doing the same? Keeping busy to avoid her thoughts? "I feel better than I have in a long time, so I'm going to hold on to that feeling as long as I can."

"Good." He nodded. "I'd better go find Judd."

Nicole joined her friends and handed them the bottles.

"...and then the woman shrieked like a peacock..." Gabby could barely hold in her laughter as she told them about one of the guests at the hotel stepping on a snake outside.

Nicole settled in next to Brittany on the couch. Last year she'd been isolated. Throughout her marriage, she'd never made friends beyond the mentor-like relationship she'd had with her boss, Delia. Look at her now. Nicole had an entire community helping her out. She had close friends who truly cared about her.

Judd came to mind, and she sighed. She'd never admit it out loud, but she was attracted to him. And the thought of going to Christmas Fest together, just the two of them, had filled her with a new kind of excitement.

When Mom started dating Steve, her eyes had sparkled with the same excitement. She'd run to her room to take Steve's calls. She'd spent hours preening and prepping to go out with him.

If it meant becoming like her mother, Nicole didn't want to be excited about going to the festival with Judd.

But Saturday wasn't a date. Judd wasn't interested in her like that.

She sighed.

That thought depressed her even more than the fear of becoming her mother.

It was fine and all to not spend every day in the fetal position grieving for Aaron, but it was an entirely other thing to be excited about spending time with another man. She'd better watch herself. She didn't want to be like her mother. And something told her with Judd she was dangerously close to it.

"What did you want to talk to me about?" Mason Fanning entered the stables wearing an almost-identical outfit to

Judd's: a black work coat, jeans and cowboy boots.

"Thanks for coming." Judd removed his leather gloves to take a break from mucking horse stalls. He'd called Mason after church and asked him if he planned on coming to Nicole's with Brittany this afternoon. When Mason answered in the affirmative, Judd had asked him if he could pick his brain about something.

"No problem, man." Mason strode over. "We're trying to support Nicole as much as possible right now."

"I'm glad she has all of you."

"We feel the same about her." Mason studied him. "She's doing better out here, you know. Your cabin…it's been good for her. I think she's healing."

Judd hoped so. He wanted her to be happy.

"We brought a few Christmas decorations over for her. Figured she might need some help getting the season's cheer in there." Mason leaned his forearm against the corner of a stall.

"How did she react?" The Christmas music hadn't gone over well yesterday, and he didn't want her upset.

"She liked it. Said it made the room cozy."

Judd had the squirrelly feeling he got whenever he wasn't sure what to say. "You want to go back to my house for a minute?"

"Nah. It's not snowing yet. I won't be able to drag Brittany away from the babies for a while. Why don't we ride?"

A man after his own heart. "You can saddle Diesel. I'll ride Candy." Judd led the way to the tack room. Then they gathered the horses and saddled them.

"I knew Diesel was big, but up close, he must be sixteen hands." Mason let out a low whistle, stroking the horse's neck. "Shiniest coat I've ever seen. Look at that color. Pure mahogany. He's a beauty."

"He is a fine piece of horseflesh. He's sweet on Candy, too, so you'll have no trouble keeping him in line."

They headed out to the far pasture where

part of the herd grazed. Under a white sky, the mountains looked purple and imposing in the distance. The wind bit at his cheeks, and he sensed the snowstorm sure to come.

As they neared the cattle, Judd slowed Candy and faced Mason. "I love this land, these animals, with every cell in my body. It's in my blood. My soul."

"I know." Mason nodded. "I feel the same about my ranch."

"That's why I wanted to talk to you." A sudden case of the nerves attacked. He didn't want to sound stupid. But Mason was a good guy, a rancher like him. Judd could trust him. He blew out a breath. "I'm trying to do some long-term planning. Estate planning. And I'm at a loss. I… I don't want the entire town knowing."

There. He'd gotten it out.

"I understand, man." Mason craned his neck to take in the vast spread. "It's hard not knowing what will happen to it."

"Exactly." His shoulders relaxed.

"Obviously, Brittany and Noah and

any future kids we have will inherit my ranch."

Judd nodded.

"But if I was in your shoes, I probably would have reached out to a neighbor to find out if they would want the additional land. The McCoys or TJ Hartford would be your best options. Your place is too far for some of the others to take over your herd."

He hadn't thought of that, but what Mason said made sense.

"If you don't want to do that, consider your best ranch hands. One of them would likely treasure this place and keep it running the way you do now." Mason patted Diesel's neck. "There's another option, too, you know. You could make it easy on yourself."

"How so?" Judd wasn't big on Cash McCoy or his older brother. They were both a little too wild and flirtatious with the ladies for his taste. And TJ Hartford's ranch had been neglected ever since the oldest boy, Rhett, left town years ago. The ranch-hand idea hadn't been Judd's favorite when Stu mentioned it, but, if push came to shove, he might have to go that route.

"Get married and have some kids," Mason said. "There are a lot of women around here who would make you happy. Most of us took over family ranches from our parents or grandparents."

His brain instantly went to Nicole.

"Eden's single," Mason continued. "And Misty and..."

The cold breeze sent a shiver down his spine. Like he needed anything else to think about. His mind was full up on things he didn't want in there. Naming an heir in his will. Being the subject of gossip around town. How much he was drawn to Nicole. How the triplets had stolen his heart.

"I don't think so." He was not getting married to Eden or Misty or...the pretty widow living down the lane.

Mason laughed. "Just giving you something to think about. Not everyone wants to raise cattle, anyhow. My son might decide to do something else when he grows up. I hope not, but I would respect his decision."

"I appreciate your suggestions," Judd said. "But I'm not getting married anytime soon."

"If you say so." Mason smirked.

He did say so. And he wasn't changing his mind.

Why was he asking these ranchers how to plan his future, anyhow? They didn't know the first thing about what he needed. He tightened his grip on the reins and wheeled Candy around to head back. He was a loner. Quiet. Reserved.

And he wasn't going to risk everything with the one woman he couldn't stand to lose.

# *Chapter Seven*

Nicole piped delicate loops of icing to represent the molding on one of the gingerbread walls Thursday after supper. Judd was currently in the living room talking to the triplets as they played in their bouncy seats. With a critical eye to her workmanship, she straightened. Delia would be proud of her. Nicole hadn't lost her decorating touch after a year away from it. This house was going to be stunning, and Judd's help was making it possible.

Every evening this week, he'd been taking care of the triplets while she decorated the walls of the house. Sometimes he sat on a stool across the counter from her and kept an eye on the babies while she piped. Other times, he soothed their cries or played with them. Last night, Eli had finally rolled over like his siblings.

Her babies were thriving here. And so was she.

Only two more days until Christmas Fest. Nicole couldn't wait. Tomorrow she'd make the cupcakes for the bake sale while Jane watched the children in the morning.

"I have to hand it to you—the walls look really nice." Judd had picked up Amelia and carried her over. "You're sure all the frosting won't get messed up when we put them together?"

"Stop worrying about it." She winked and stepped back, pastry bag in hand, to survey the finished wall. A few lines were shaky, but overall, the Victorian details were spot-on. "You'll have to trust me on this."

"I figured you put the walls together first and decorate it last."

"My boss was an expert gingerbread-house maker. She won competitions. People drove from other towns to see her displays. She taught me all her secrets."

"Okay, I trust you. And I have to admit, I never thought you'd be able to do all this and take care of three babies." He looked down at Amelia and tickled under her chin. The baby giggled, and Nicole's heart flip-flopped. It did every time she saw him interacting with the babies. He was so good with them. And they seemed to love him right back.

"I couldn't have done it without your help." She bent to inspect the window-panes. "If you weren't entertaining them, these walls would be bare."

"I'm not doing much."

He always said that. And Nicole didn't get it. He'd helped her change their diapers on more than one occasion. Moved them to their bouncy seats or the play mat when they got tired and antsy. Given them their pacifiers when they cranked. He did a lot. More than most guys would.

Why hadn't one of the local women snatched this hunky family man up?

"Judd?" She shouldn't ask, but they'd been getting to know each other better all week and she needed to know. "How is it that you've never been married?"

He started coughing, his face growing red.

"I'm sorry." Her and her big mouth. What if he'd been engaged, or a girlfriend had broken his heart? She should have left well enough alone. "It's none of my business."

"I'm not like you." He didn't meet her eyes.

What did he mean by that? She set the pastry bag down and gave him her full attention. "O-kay."

"I'm not like any of you."

Now she really didn't know what he meant. "You don't want to get married? You like being alone?"

"I'm comfortable being alone. I'm not comfortable being around other people all the time."

Was decorating with her a sacrifice he was making for his aunt and nothing more? She'd thought he was enjoying their time together the way she was.

"Well, in a few more weeks you won't have to do this. The house will be finished." She hated even thinking that far ahead. She liked having supper with him, and she really liked having him here while she worked on his aunt's gift. After Christmas they'd still eat together, but there wouldn't be a reason for him to stick around. Maybe he was counting down the days until he could have his evenings to himself again.

And why wouldn't he? What guy wanted to babysit and change diapers while watching someone pipe icing? It couldn't be a thrill for him.

"I don't *have* to do this, Nicole," he said quietly. "I want to."

His simple statement blossomed in her heart like a prairie full of wildflowers in the spring.

He wanted to be with her?

She wanted to be with him, too.

Not that this was romantic or anything. It wasn't. Couldn't be.

"I'm glad," she said. "If I feel like a chore, please don't think you have to keep doing this." A few years ago, she'd begged Aaron to come to the Christmas open house at the bakery. Delia had put three of Nicole's gingerbread buildings into the front window showcase. Aaron had told her he'd be working late, and she'd gotten upset. It had taken her three days to work up the courage to tell him how much it would mean to her if he came. He arrived minutes before the store closed and barely looked at the gingerbread city scene she and Delia had worked so hard on.

She'd been a chore that night.

She never wanted to feel like one again.

"You could never be a chore." Judd shifted Amelia to his other arm and stared at Nicole with those deep blue eyes. Sincerity radiated from him. "I haven't gotten married because I keep to myself. I don't know what women want, and by the time they realize that, they're fed up with me and leave."

"Maybe you haven't found the right one."

"Yeah, well, I'm getting up there in years." He shrugged. "You're young. You have lots of time left."

"You're not exactly a grandpa." She attempted to laugh, but it fell flat. "I mean, you're not even forty yet, are you?"

"No." He frowned. "But I'm set in my ways. Marriage isn't for me."

Fair enough. He was warning her not to get too close. She'd told herself the same thing time and again, but…

Her heart didn't seem to be listening.

She'd already had the heartbreak of a lifetime. Maybe Judd was doing her a favor.

Either way, Nicole didn't have much choice.

The following afternoon Judd paid a visit to the McCoy Ranch. Cash was repairing a section of wooden rail on a corral as Judd stomped through the snow.

"You want some help with that?" Judd called.

Cash grinned and waved him over. The air was cold and smelled like cattle, but it had stopped snowing this morning and there wasn't any more snow in the forecast until next week.

"Stupid steers ganged together and took out this fence. Have to round 'em up in a minute."

"You know where they are?" Judd grabbed the other end of a plank of wood and helped him carry it to the broken section. He held it in place while Cash screwed it to the post.

"I have a pretty good idea." Cash straightened and pointed to a herd of cattle in the distance. "The cows are all working on a line of feed. My guess is the steers busted out to join them."

Judd noted the deep grooves in the snow from where the tractor had driven. "How are you getting out there?"

"I don't want to risk my horses. I'll take a UTV."

"Do you want some company? I can help." Judd surveyed the corral. "You going to put some feed in their trough? They won't give you any trouble if they have some food when they come back."

"Smart thinking."

A little while later, they'd located the five steers. Those boys knew they were in trouble and branched off from the cows automatically. Judd couldn't help chuckling as they trotted back to their pen. They had the air of teenagers caught skipping school but high-fiving each other, knowing it had been worth it.

Once Cash closed the gate behind the steers, he grinned. "Thanks. I appreciate the help. That was pretty easy."

"Looks like I was here at the right time."

"What's on your mind, Judd?" Cash led the way back to a pole barn. Judd fell in beside him.

"Your dad doesn't ranch anymore, does he?"

Cash opened the door and shook his

head. Inside was marginally warmer than outdoors.

"Just you and Chris running it, huh?" Judd asked.

"Yeah, you could say that." Cash grimaced. "Do you see Chris around, though?"

"No." Was it a trick question? He hadn't seen any sign of Cash's older brother.

"Neither do I." He grabbed a broom and swept up loose hay. "I'm fed up with him."

"Where is he?"

Cash shrugged. "The bar. The bank. Laramie. Timbuktu. Who knows anymore?"

"He's not helping here?"

"He used to." Cash pushed the hay into the corner, turned back to face him and leaned on the handle of the broom. "We haven't exactly been getting along."

"Is this new?" He hadn't realized Cash was bearing the brunt of the ranch work.

"Three years now." Cash took off his gloves. "Why? Did you need to see him?"

"No, but you've got me curious. How is this affecting the place?"

"It's fine." Cash didn't meet his eyes. "I'm holding it down fine."

"But it's not only your responsibility."

"I know. I'm going to have to talk to my dad soon." The bravado in Cash's expression dissolved. Regret replaced it. "I want to take this ranch to the next level, but my hands are tied because of Chris. Something's got to give."

Judd didn't like the sound of that. "Would you walk away?"

"Don't want to. But I'm not going to work my fingers to the bone so Chris can fritter away our livelihood on booze and gambling, either."

"I don't blame you." He wished he had something to say that would help, but he didn't know what would.

Cash set the broom to the side. "I know you didn't come here to talk about me and my problems. What can I help you with?"

"If you can work it out with your brother, will you still want to ranch?" Judd asked.

"This land, these cattle, it's all I know. Ranching is in my blood."

It was the first time Judd could remember Cash being so transparent. He was usually the life of the party, flirting with the girls and making everyone laugh. Frankly, Judd liked this Cash much better than the one he presented to the public.

"I hear you on that." Judd nodded. It was all he knew, too. "Is there anything I can do to help?"

"Nah." Cash grinned, and the transparency disappeared behind his fun-loving mask. "It'll be fine. You caught me at a bad moment, that's all."

Judd hesitated, wanting to help, to say something reassuring. But he didn't know what. "Text me anytime you need an extra set of hands."

"Thanks. Same to you."

With that, Judd nodded and trudged back to his truck.

It didn't seem fair that Cash was stuck with all the work while his brother did whatever he wanted. And if Judd had to guess, they split the profits evenly. He'd probably be upset, too, if he had a brother who wasn't pulling his weight.

Maybe naming Cash in his will was an option Judd could consider at this point in his life. Cash might have a reputation with the ladies, but his ranching skills were never in question. As Judd grew older, he would need to think about passing the ranch down to someone younger, but for now, Cash was a solid choice.

As he stepped up into his truck, a flurry of snowflakes came down. He hoped the meteorologist hadn't been mistaken about the clear forecast. If more snow fell tonight, there was a good chance Christmas Fest would be canceled tomorrow.

All week he'd been looking forward to taking Nicole to the festival. He started his truck and backed up to turn around. As he drove down the long driveway, he kept hearing Stu's and Mason's advice to get married and have kids.

The other night when Nicole had asked him about marriage, he'd been up-front with her. Naturally, his words hadn't come out right, and she'd taken them to mean he considered spending time with her a chore. A chore. He shook his head. She and those babies were the highlight of his day. He raced through his ranch duties to freshen up before he came over each night. And he was getting better at caring for the triplets while she squeezed those tiny lines of frosting onto the gingerbread walls.

No, Nicole Taylor was no chore.

He just hoped no one in town noticed his level-ten crush on her tomorrow. He could handle being embarrassed for his own sake, but he didn't want anyone talking about her because of him. Christmas Fest could be great, or it could be a disaster. There was only one way to find out.

# Chapter Eight

"Wow, I can't believe how much bigger this is than I remembered." Nicole strolled next to Judd in downtown Rendezvous the next day. Centennial Street had been blocked off with food trucks and various vendors lining it. Evergreen boughs and red ribbons were hung everywhere. Down the street, the large park had been converted into a winter wonderland with reindeer, Santa's workshop and hot chocolate stands next to a skating rink.

She was *so* ready for Christmas Fest.

No babies. No worries. Just an afternoon to be like any other twentysomething woman for once.

"I haven't been here in years." Judd took her elbow as a couple of teenagers almost ran into them. He pointed to a side street. "Rec center's down this way."

"You really don't mind checking out the bake sale?" She peeked at him, needing to see his reaction for herself. Aaron hadn't enjoyed these types of events, and Nicole had never dated anyone else—not that this was a date—so she wasn't sure if she was boring Judd or not.

"Why would I mind?" His smile made his eyes dance. "It's what Christmas Fest is all about."

For this not being a date, she'd spent far too much time putting on her makeup and curling her hair during the babies' morning nap. Then she'd dug through her winter items to find the cute knit hat she'd purchased a few years ago. The one with a fluffy pom-pom on top. It had matching gloves, too.

She still hadn't lost the baby weight, so she'd squeezed into her stretchiest jeans and found a long sweater to cover any lumps. It was funny, though, that she didn't feel self-conscious at all with Judd. She felt…excited. It was nice to get out of the house and have some fun without having to worry about the babies or the other things tangling her heart.

"Nicole!" Waving furiously, Linda Mulroney headed in their direction. Linda was one of Mom's good friends. The bubbly woman held her toddler grandson's hand as she approached them. "Well, look at you out and about. How's your mom? She hasn't called me in a few days."

"I haven't talked to her, either, but she seemed great the last time she called." Which had been a few weeks ago, if Nicole's memory served her correctly. She really should reach out to her mother soon.

Linda gave Judd a sly glance then focused on Nicole again. "Have you two gone skating yet?"

Nicole glanced up at Judd. "I'm not sure we're going to."

"Well, when you have a babysitter, you shouldn't waste a precious minute. That's my motto, anyway." Linda winked at her. "Want me to snap a picture of you two and send it to your mom?"

"No!" Nicole didn't mean to shout. Even Judd looked taken aback. "We're actually on our way to the bake sale. See you later."

"Have fun, you two." Linda wiggled her fingers in a wave.

How mortifying. No doubt, Linda was texting Mom at this very moment with news that Nicole was on a date with Judd. A sick feeling landed in her tummy. What would people think? Most likely they'd assume she was like her mother. Except worse. Because Nicole should still be grieving and not having fun with Judd Wilson.

She marched forward. Judd easily kept pace with her.

Should she still be grieving? Hadn't she cried enough? When would it be acceptable for her to move forward?

"We don't have to do this, you know." Judd's low voice startled her.

"I want to." And she did. She desperately wanted to enjoy this day. If Linda got the wrong impression, oh, well. Nicole couldn't be a grieving widow forever. "Being here feels..." She raised her eyebrows. "Normal. And my life hasn't felt normal in a long time."

The muscle in his cheek flickered, but he nodded. "Whatever you'd like to do, just say the word, and if it gets too much, I'll take you home."

"I want to see if anyone's bought my cupcakes." She'd made three dozen in different flavors yesterday. Just thinking about them improved her mood.

"You made cupcakes?" Their boots crunched on the salt sprinkled over the sidewalks. "When did you find time to do that?"

"Yesterday morning. Jane Boyd comes on Fridays, and she practically pushes me out of the living room so she can take charge of the babies."

"And you're okay with that?"

"Okay with it?" She laughed. The crisp air and faint sound of jingle bells added a spring to her step. "Are you kidding? I love it. It gives me time for myself without feeling guilty."

The rec center's double doors were up ahead. A steady stream of people entered and exited. When it was their turn, Judd held the door open. Two boys raced under his arm outside. "If you were making stuff for the bake sale, it wasn't really time for yourself."

"Baking *is* time for myself."

"You're something, you know that?"

She'd always thought of herself as ordinary. For him to pay her that compliment meant more than he could know.

The brightly lit room buzzed with conversation. Kids in snowsuits darted around their parents, and tables had been placed around the perimeter. A children's crafts area took up a portion of the room. Nicole caught a glimpse of two little girls coloring at one of the tables. One day her little ones would color at Christmas Fest and run around with their friends. She tried to picture them a little older and couldn't. They were still so tiny.

"Bake sale's this way." Judd jerked his thumb to the back of the room.

Nicole stayed by his side, pausing now and then to check out homemade candles and other displays. Cinnamon and coffee permeated the air, and her stomach grumbled. As soon as they scoped out the bake sale, she needed a bite to eat.

"My kind of display." Judd rubbed his hands together in front of two long tables covered in red tablecloths. Brittany, Mason and Brittany's grandmother sat behind them.

"Hey, you two. I hope you brought your wallets." Brittany flourished her hand over the spread with the skill of a game-show host. Nicole noted a variety of pies, cookies and brownies. What she didn't see were her cupcakes. Hadn't anyone put them out?

"I made cupcakes," Nicole said. "But I don't see them."

Brittany's long blond hair curled over

her shoulders, and her stunning blue eyes sparkled. "Not only were they the first items displayed, but Lois told me they were the first to sell out. I've had several people stop back to get your information. I hope you don't mind me telling them you baked them."

People liked her cupcakes! A thrill zinged down her spine. She wanted to do a happy dance on the spot. "Mind? Why would I mind? They really liked them?"

Mason patted his stomach. "I know I did. What kind had the tan frosting and cinnamon on top?"

"Pumpkin with cream cheese. I also made dark chocolate with cookies-and-cream frosting, and a salted caramel white cupcake."

"The only complaint we've gotten…" Mason said. Nicole's gut clenched. People had complained? "There weren't enough of them."

Her breath came out in a whoosh. "Really? Oh, you just made my day." She clapped her hands together and turned to Judd. "They liked the cupcakes."

"Why wouldn't they? Everything you make is delicious."

Somehow having his approval was even better than the cupcakes selling out. She turned away, but his image was burned into her mind. His tall, powerful frame. The twinkle in his eyes. The patience that permeated him. The tiny gap between his teeth. The slight graying at his temples.

All it would take was the barest whisper for her to fall hard for Judd Wilson.

But the other night he'd spelled it out for her—he was set in his ways. He had no plans to get married.

*Married?* She shook herself out of the alternate reality she'd momentarily found herself in.

No one was talking marriage. No one was talking love or relationships or anything.

Only someone like her mom would get stars in her eyes so soon after being widowed. And Judd wasn't interested in her.

He'd been kind to her, yes, but she couldn't mistake kindness for romantic feelings.

"Should we continue on?" She waved goodbye to Brittany and Mason. "I'd like to check out the food trucks. I'm hungry."

"This way." Judd placed his hand at the small of her back and ushered her toward the side door. His touch seared all the way through her coat and sweater.

If the slightest touch was affecting her this way, maybe she should seriously work on getting her feelings back to friend mode.

It wasn't as if she was in love with him or anything. When the gingerbread house was finished, they wouldn't be hanging out as much, and this crush would fade away. She wouldn't waste another minute thinking about it. It was time to enjoy the rest of the afternoon.

Judd held a paper cup filled with apple slices as Nicole reached out to feed the reindeer. All day he'd been getting wrapped tighter and tighter into the

Christmas Fest spirit. Nicole had been a big part of it. Her expression had been priceless when Brittany told her the cupcakes had sold out. She'd looked shocked, then in utter awe. He'd fought the urge to take her into his arms and hug her right off her feet.

That would have been a disaster.

It was bad enough they'd been getting double takes and whispers all afternoon. Nicole didn't seem to notice, but he did. And the resulting emotions were churning his stomach. That and the barbecue they'd eaten a few hours ago.

It hadn't been a good idea to take her around the festival. People assumed they were a couple, and they weren't. Plus, it was glaringly obvious he was not her type. For one, there was his age. For another, she was so bright and friendly to everyone, and he was...not. There were other reasons as well, even if he couldn't name them at the moment.

Still, he'd promised her they would do whatever she wanted. So they'd attempted to ice-skate. It had not gone well. But he'd held her hand the third time she fell as she dissolved into laughter, and he'd always cherish the memory.

"Next year the babies will be walking." She took another apple slice out of the cup he held. Her cheeks were pink from the cold, and she had a sparkle about her. His mouth grew dry. If there had been mistletoe nearby, he would have been tempted to kiss her. "I'm kind of looking forward to starting my own traditions with them. We'll sprinkle glittery reindeer food on the lawn on Christmas Eve and leave special cookies by the fireplace. And I know they're going to love Christmas Fest. I can't wait until they're old enough to do the crafts and get their pictures with Santa."

She'd said *we'll*. Did that mean she was including him? Or was it a general thing? Because he'd been able to picture himself doing all of those things with her and the triplets. And, more than that, he wanted to.

All of his life, he'd liked the idea of having a wife and kids, but he'd never actually seen himself having them. Until Nicole came along.

"Nicole!" Mrs. Jenkins, a retired schoolteacher, shoved through a group of teens to stand before them. She held something in her hand. "I'm glad I finally caught you. I saw you earlier and rushed back home to get these pictures. I was looking through old photographs a few weeks ago and came across these. I figured you'd want them." The corners of her mouth tugged down in sympathy.

"Thank you." Nicole took the small stack of pictures, glanced at them and blanched. Judd wondered what was on them for her mood to change so quickly.

Mrs. Jenkins patted her hand. "I'm sure this holiday season has been hard on you. We're all thinking of you and those babies. We loved Aaron. He was one of my favorite students. It's a shame he was taken so young."

"Yes." Her voice sounded strangled. "It is."

"It's good to see you here, Nicole." With

a sympathetic look, the woman turned and left.

Nicole stared at the pictures in her hand. Judd was pretty sure he could reach out and touch the air of dejection surrounding her. One of the pictures floated to the ground. He bent to pick it up.

Nicole's smiling face as a teenager beamed back at him. A tall blond kid—handsome, with a cocky smile—had his arm around her shoulders. They looked like they fit together. The perfect couple.

Fumbling, he handed it to her. "Here."

She slid them all into her coat pocket and shivered, her eyes blank. "Can we get out of here?"

"Yes." He tried to usher her forward, but she stepped away from his touch.

He clenched his jaw. He'd been fooling himself with all this together time. Worse, Nicole was supposed to be enjoying herself, but her day had been ruined.

They strode in silence past the food trucks and happy families. Christmas music came from the sidewalk. All afternoon he'd felt like he belonged at the festival. He'd enjoyed the activities and been comfortable by Nicole's side. And now he felt detached from it all.

Christmas Fest, like most other social events he attended, was for other people. Not for him.

When they reached the side road where they'd parked a few blocks down, Nicole stopped in her tracks.

"What's the matter?" he asked.

"I shouldn't be doing this." Tears formed in her eyes.

She could only mean him.

"What kind of person am I?" She met his eyes, and he was struck by the pain in them. "I'm running around a festival having fun without my babies. A year ago, I was holding Aaron's hand while we waited for test results. And today I haven't thought about him at all, Judd. Not once. I… I feel sick."

She swayed, and Judd wrapped his arm around her shoulders to keep her upright.

"Easy does it. Do you think you're

going to pass out?" He was surprised he sounded so calm, because inside he was quaking. Everything she said nailed to his conscience.

"No, I'm not physically sick. I'm..." She straightened, her eyes imploring him. "I'm a horrible person."

"Don't. Don't do that. None of this..." He stared up at the sky, trying desperately to find the right words. How could he make her understand? "None of this is your fault. Your husband died, and I know you loved him. The whole town knows it. And those pictures—you guys just looked right together. But you've had an awful year. You deserve to come out and enjoy yourself. You can have a life, too. You have nothing to be ashamed of."

Shaking her head, she started walking again. She wiped under her eyes. He didn't want her to cry. He'd do just about anything to take away her pain.

"I don't want to be like my mom." She seemed to grow taller as she marched forward.

"What do you mean?"

"She's never happy unless she's with a man."

"What does that have to do with you?"

"I will not turn into her. My kids are number one in my life, and I never want them to think otherwise."

"No one would ever think that, let alone your children."

"Oh, yeah?" She stopped and turned to face him. "Tell that to Mom's friend Linda, who stopped us earlier. Tell that to Mrs. Jenkins. They probably think I'm trying to wrap you around my finger."

"You?" He let out a nervous laugh. "No one would think that. If anything, they'd think less of me."

She shook her head as if he'd said something idiotic. "I don't think so."

He had to be honest with her. "I'm a good ten years older than you. It's off-putting for people to see an older guy with a beautiful young widow."

Her mouth dropped open. Then her eyes clouded. She rolled her eyes. "When are you going to get it in your head you're not an old man? My word. No one thinks it's weird for us to be together at Christmas Fest for any reason other than the fact I should be mourning, not living it up."

Part of him wanted to pump his fist in the air that she didn't seem to see their age difference as a problem. But the other part couldn't forget the picture of her and Aaron. They'd looked right together. They had history. Children.

She'd never feel for Judd what he felt for her. It was time to put a stop to this attraction to her before his heart got buried for good.

## Chapter Nine

Things between her and Judd had been strained all week.

Wednesday evening, Nicole piped a thick swirl of chocolate frosting onto the final dozen cupcakes Mrs. Beverly requested. Orders for holiday cookie trays and pies had been coming in since Sunday. Word about her baking had hit Rendezvous like a sudden snowstorm. And she was glad. It would be the perfect way for her to earn income. For now, at least. Maybe someday she'd even open her own bakery.

Baking was a welcome distraction from

her current problems. Ever since the words *beautiful young widow* had come out of Judd's mouth on Saturday, she'd replayed them again and again.

He thought she was beautiful?

She didn't feel beautiful. She'd always just been Aaron's girlfriend. Then Aaron's wife. So for Judd to call her beautiful? Well, it had been heady.

With a final flourish of her pastry bag, she finished the cupcakes and liberally sprinkled red and green nonpareils over them before carefully placing them into a white cardboard box.

With a big yawn, she worked the kinks out of her neck, then wiped the counter and washed the decorator tip in sudsy water. Her pajamas were calling her name.

Her cell phone rang. The screen showed that it was Mom. As she headed down the hall to her bedroom, she answered it. "How's Florida?"

"Overcast today, but it was sixty-two, so I'll take it. How are the babies?"

"They're great. They had a checkup on Tuesday, and they're all gaining weight."

"Even Amelia?"

"Yes, just not as much as the boys." Propping the phone between her ear and shoulder, she opened her dresser drawers to find her favorite pajamas.

"Did you have any trouble getting them to the appointment? Or did Judd help you? Linda told me how cozy you two looked at Christmas Fest. Atta girl."

How did one respond to that? She wished she could think of a snappy reply off the top of her head like Gabby would, but she settled for the truth. "We went as friends."

"Sure, Nicki. Just keep going as friends and you'll do fine."

Irritation boiled over. "I'm not like that."

"Like what?" She sounded taken aback.

*Like you.* "It was a way to get out of the house. Nothing more."

"Well, I suppose he is older than you. Aren't you attracted to him a little?"

*Yes. Too much.* "He's happy being single, and I'm not..." She almost said *ready*, but she wasn't sure if that was true. Part of her felt ready. She'd taken so many steps this year, and now that she was getting all these bakery orders, she wasn't as worried about her future.

"Okay, okay, I get it. You're not over Aaron. I understand. He could have proposed to you in third grade and you would have accepted. But at some point it's okay to admit he's gone and there might be another Mr. Right for you."

For the first time in ages, her mom had said something useful. "Do you think so?"

"I know so. Look at me. Steve and I are having so much fun. I have two job interviews coming up, and he starts working for a cooling company next week. It's all working out."

"It's a little different for me." Nicole scrunched her nose in distaste. She had no desire to just *have fun* with a guy. She wanted steadiness, a commitment. Her mom had dated several men over the years. When Nicole was young, she'd clung to the guys, believing they would be her new daddy. But none of them lasted. And in some ways, it had jaded her.

"I can see you aren't going to listen to me." Mom let out a disgruntled sigh. "Have you talked to Stella?"

"No, I haven't. I called a few times and texted, but she only texts me back short replies."

"I finally got ahold of her this week. Looks like she's dating the owner of the swanky hotel where she's working."

Nicole's spirits sank. For years, her little sister had taken after their mother, and it hadn't led her to lasting happiness.

"He's taking her to Europe in January. Can you believe that? She's done good for herself…"

Nicole couldn't listen to her mother rave about Stella's poor choices as if they were a good thing. "I think one of the babies needs me. I've got to go."

"Okay. Kiss them for me."

"I will."

Her mother hung up first, and Nicole

tossed the phone on the bed. She thought about Stella up in Vancouver, dating some bigwig she worked for. It didn't seem like a good situation. In fact, it sounded an awful lot like Mom's current situation, except with a guy who had money. She wanted to warn her sister to take it slow, to get to know the guy before flying off to Europe with him. But Stella never listened to her.

After putting on her pajamas, Nicole padded to the living room, plopped down on the couch and sighed. Who was she to talk? She'd been spending a lot of time with Judd, and yes, she'd gotten to know him all year, but this arrangement of theirs added an intimacy she hadn't been prepared for.

Every day she planned meals she thought he might like. She counted down the minutes until supper, anticipating when he'd knock on the door. Earlier this evening, she'd finished piping the moldings onto all the walls and sent the decorated walls home with him so Gretchen wouldn't see them when she helped with the triplets.

Nicole had gotten close to Judd in a very short amount of time. Just like her mom. Just like Stella.

Her in-laws would be here in two days. What if they picked up on her feelings toward Judd? She couldn't bear to have them think less of her.

She crushed a throw pillow into her stomach.

Why was life so complicated?

Judd had been trying to distract himself from Nicole all week. It wasn't easy. Thursday morning he finished checking cattle and looked up at the sky. Blue without a cloud in sight. The snow from last week was packed down, making it easy to navigate on horseback. He'd decided today was the day to find out what Dallas and Clay would do if they owned his property. If either of their answers pleased him, he'd seriously consider naming one of them in his will.

Dallas circled his horse around the herd and came back to where Judd sat on Candy.

"All set?" Judd asked.

"All accounted for."

Clay rode up, too. "Green tag 338 looks good today."

"I'm glad to hear it. She worried me on Monday. I'd hate to see her lose the calf she's carrying."

They compared notes on the overall health of the herd before turning to head back.

Judd wanted to have his estate plan settled before the new year, but it was looking less and less likely each day he wasted trying to figure out who would be the best person to leave the ranch to.

Every night he prayed for guidance, but he still didn't know what to do.

Earlier this week, he'd talked to an estate lawyer who put him in contact with a wealthy big-game hunter known for preserving land. Judd had no intention of seeing his property get converted from cattle ranching to big-game hunting. However, Dallas or Clay might feel differently, and if they did, it would affect his decision.

"You guys ever hear of Jim Reed?" Judd glanced from side to side as each cowboy flanked him.

"Is he a country singer?" Dallas, a lanky twenty-eight-year-old, glanced his way.

"Sounds like that NFL coach. No, wait. I'm thinking of Andy Reid." Clay, the more serious of the two, was a large man with a full beard.

"He's a big-game hunter. He's looking for a property like mine. I talked to him a few days ago."

"You're not selling the place, are you?" Clay's bushy eyebrows furrowed.

Judd straightened. Maybe Clay felt the connection to the land, too.

"If the price is right, he is." Dallas guffawed.

That was what he'd been afraid of. Dollar signs could sway a person.

"I have no plans to sell the ranch." Judd

sat tall in his saddle. “Even if Jim rattled off a seven-figure offer. Would you?”

“Seven figures, huh?” Clay gripped the reins with his leather-gloved hands.

“I’d sign that deal as soon as he set it on the table,” Dallas said. Judd wasn’t surprised.

“What about you, Clay?” Judd held out hope the man would defend the ranch. “It would mean selling off the herd.”

“I can’t work cattle forever.” Clay shivered. “I’d sell. Buy a few acres so I could keep my horse and retire young. Yes, that’s what I would do. But, boss, we know you aren’t the type to retire. Sometimes I think these cows are your family, you dote on ’em so much. You wouldn’t sell this place in a million years.”

It was true. Judd faced straight ahead, not wanting either cowboy to see how disappointed he was. But hadn’t he known this all along? No one loved this land the way he did. Dallas and Clay were his employees, hired hands, and they didn’t own the ranch or bear the responsibility when a calf died or a drought hit. He couldn't expect them to be as emotionally invested in this place as he was.

But it didn't take away his disappointment.

At Christmas Fest, he'd been struck by Nicole's statement that enjoying the festival made her feel normal. He knew exactly what she meant. He'd been trying to feel normal his entire life, and for the past few weeks, he'd gotten a glimpse of what it felt like.

Being around her made him feel normal. Like any other guy.

All week she'd been quiet. He'd watched her take her time decorating every gingerbread wall, and the sections all sat in his kitchen waiting to be assembled. Next week was Christmas, and his gingerbread days with Nicole would be over.

Maybe it was better this way. He enjoyed spending time with Nicole and the babies too much. Last Saturday had brought him back to reality—she wasn't his and never would be. He'd better make peace with it soon or he might never return to his own kind of normal. And then where would he be?

"Your packages arrived." Judd carried two large boxes stacked on top of each other into Nicole's cabin at supper time. He set them along the wall next to the door. "There are three more in my truck. I'll be right back."

"Thank you!" Nicole wiped her hands on a dish towel, took a pair of scissors out from the drawer and hurried to the boxes. She'd ordered pale pink and mint-green candies to finish decorating the gingerbread house once she and Judd assembled it. She'd also ordered several Christmas gifts and fancy cardboard containers for her baked items. Presenting a professional package to her clients was important to her.

Mrs. Beverly had picked up her cupcakes this morning and oohed and aahed over the babies. She'd made an offhand comment about how they made everything triply sweet, and Nicole had been mulling over the phrase ever since.

Triply Sweet. Had a nice ring to it. It would make a catchy name for her home business.

Judd came back inside with another large box, set it next to the other two and left again.

She sliced through the packing tape of the first box and peeked inside. Baby toys—three of each—scarves for her girlfriends and a gorgeous plaid wool blanket for Judd. She closed the flaps and hauled the box to her bedroom so he wouldn't see his gift. It had been a splurge, but the red, black and gray blanket had looked manly and warm and perfect for him. He'd done so much for her.

Amelia started crying from her bouncy seat near the dining table, so Nicole picked her up and carried her over to the other boxes.

"That's the last of them." Judd set the final two on the floor, took off his coat and boots and joined her. He held out his index finger to Amelia, and she wrapped her tiny hand around it. She was still fussy, but at least she wasn't crying.

Judd's cheeks were red from the cold. There was an air of vigor and strength about the man that was way too appealing. Amelia held up her little arms for him to take her. Her baby girl sure liked Judd. It was hard not to.

With the scissors, Nicole opened the next box. "Oh, good!" She took out plastic baggies filled with candies shaped like silver stars, flat sugar discs and itty-bitty snowflake sprinkles. "We can add these to the house after we put it together next week."

"I thought we were putting it together this Saturday." He frowned.

"My in-laws will be here. If we attach the walls and roof on Monday and Tuesday, we can add the final decorations on Wednesday. Since Christmas Eve is Thursday, I figure you'll want it ready before then."

"Right."

She opened the other boxes. Thankfully, the baking supplies and containers hadn't been damaged. She lifted them out. "Just what I needed."

"You sure you aren't working too hard?"

"I'm glad to be working at all. It's scary not having an income. It's not that I'm broke, but—" she shrugged, dusting off her knees as she stood "—I'm in charge now, and I don't have anyone to fall back on."

"You have me." He flushed. "And your friends."

"I know, and I'm thankful. But it's not the same as when Aaron was alive." She was glad she'd been frugal as his salary had grown. She'd never gotten used to having many extras. "Well, supper's ready. Let's eat."

They went to the table and sat down. The boys were kicking their legs in their bouncy seats and letting out little grunts. Her sweet boys.

Judd still held Amelia. He was talking to her in his low cowboy voice, and the baby stared at him with her mouth in an O. The sight was so dear, Nicole had to look away. Her children deserved to have a daddy who would love them.

A daddy? Where was her head at?

"Want me to say grace?" he asked. She nodded.

After the prayer, she bit into her baked chicken with too much force. Her in-laws were on their way into town tomorrow. She wasn't sure how she'd handle seeing them.

Would Lance and Sherry treat her the way they always had? Would they accept her decision to do home baking and live out here in this cabin instead of in town? They'd always been supportive. But that was when Aaron had been alive. How would they react to her new life?

For a split second she didn't want them to come. They were bound to remind her of everything she'd lost.

She washed down the bite of chicken with a drink of water.

Ready or not, she'd survive the visit.

Then she'd only have one more big worry. Getting through Christmas.

She wished she could close her eyes and wake up to the day *after* Christmas. She'd never looked forward to getting through the holidays as much as she did this one. If she could make it through the one-year anniversary of Aaron's death, she could make it through anything. Even her inconvenient feelings for Judd.

missed you so much." She knelt to pick up Eli. "See, Lance, he looks just like Aaron as a baby."

Sherry rose, holding Eli, and sidled up next to her husband. Sadness flashed in his eyes. "He sure does. This is Eli, right?"

"Yes," Nicole said, trying to ignore the sudden pressure in her chest. "Henry's hair is darker."

Feeling oddly protective of Henry, Nicole scooped him up and joined them. Lance held out his hands to take the boy, and she felt a little better. She picked up Amelia while they talked in baby voices to the boys. It would have been comical if Nicole wasn't so nervous.

After a few minutes, they all sat down. Sherry still cuddled Eli, Lance pretended to fly Henry while making airplane noises and Nicole kept Amelia on her lap.

"How are you doing? It's got to be tough with your mom no longer around." Sherry's gray eyes gleamed with sympathy. "I'm sorry you've had to move and deal with all of this on your own."

"I'm doing okay." Nicole glanced at both of them, hoping they'd see a confident young mother. "I've had a lot of help."

Sherry's lips pursed and a slight frown marred her forehead. "Yes, we heard Judd Wilson has been quite attentive."

What did she mean by *attentive*? The way she said it made it sound like an accusation. Nicole stiffened.

"We passed his house on the way in." Lance kept his focus on Henry. "It's big. Not sure why one guy needs that much space. Do you spend much time there?"

What were they implying?

"No, I don't," Nicole said. "I kind of have my hands full here with the triplets all the time."

But she did have supper with him most nights. Was that bad?

"Oh, we know," Sherry assured her. "It surprised us, I guess, to hear he's taking you to church and that you went to the festival together."

"There's no reason for us both to drive into town on Sundays." Nicole tried to melt the ice in her tone without quite succeeding. "And I baked cupcakes for the festival's bake sale."

"Right." Lance nodded. "We want to make sure you aren't rushing into anything."

"Rushing? Well, the bake sales have been sudden, but I'm managing fine."

"We meant with Judd," Sherry said.

Nicole couldn't remember the last time she'd been this mortified. What had the people of Rendezvous been telling her in-laws about her and Judd? Probably that the apple didn't fall far from the tree as far as Nicole and her mother were concerned.

"I'm sure it's all innocent." Sherry scrunched her nose at Eli. "We know how devoted you were to Aaron. Maybe Judd has the wrong idea. It's not your fault."

"He doesn't have the wrong idea. He's been very kind to me." She wanted to tell them he refused to take rent and that he was the reason she finally felt like she had a chance at making it on her own. But they might read the worst into it, and Judd didn't deserve that. "I think maybe you're the ones who have the wrong idea."

Sherry's face noticeably pinched as she gave Lance a sidelong glance. "We know how difficult it is to be raising three babies on your own. Isn't baking on top of that too much?"

"I enjoy baking." Nicole shifted Amelia to her other arm. "Some of the ladies from church have been taking turns coming in for a few hours every weekday morning. It's been great, so there's no need to worry about me." She needed to change the subject—and fast. "How is everyone? Alyssa's pregnant again, right? How are Jaycee, Tom and their little ones doing? Fill me in."

"They're all good. Alyssa still has a few months to go before the baby's due. Jaycee's kiddos keep us really busy since she's been on crutches. Of course, we're all having a hard time picturing Christmas without Aaron."

"I am, too," Nicole said quietly. Now that she had so much help, it was getting easier to think about the holidays, but she couldn't remember the last Christmas she hadn't celebrated with Aaron. Even when they were younger, she'd spent part of the day with his family. This year would be completely new.

"It's going to be hard on all of us." Sherry's voice cracked. "I hope it's okay we're having the babies' presents shipped here. We couldn't fit them in our suitcases."

"Whatever is easiest. It's kind of you."

Lance cleared his throat. "We thought we could order a pizza tonight, if that's all right with you."

"I'm always up for pizza." Nicole tried to lighten the somber mood with her cheeriest tone, but it didn't quite work.

"So what are you doing about a Christmas tree?" Sherry asked.

She gulped. She was doing nothing about a Christmas tree. "Oh, I don't need one."

"Everyone needs a Christmas tree. I know it's hard this year, but celebrating the holidays will get easier with time."

Sherry tsk-tsked. "Lance, why don't you pick up an artificial tree in town when you get the pizza later?"

"I'll do one better and go now." He got to his feet. "Where should I put Henry?"

"I'll take him." Nicole waved him over and settled Henry on her lap with Amelia. "But it really isn't necessary. I don't need a tree."

"Nonsense." Sherry scoffed. "We might not be around to help much, but we can get a tree for you."

Lance was already lacing up his boots. "I'll get your lights and decorations out when I get back. Just point me in their direction."

Nicole could still picture the dumpster where all of her Christmas items had ended up, and a dark cloud crossed over her heart. She couldn't tell them she'd thrown them all away.

The garland, twinkle lights and snowmen on the fireplace mantel caught her eye. The display from her friends had been making the holiday season a little brighter. Maybe a tree wouldn't be so bad. It would give Lance something to do. Her father-in-law liked to be busy.

"You might want to pick up a few boxes of cheap lights and bulbs," Nicole said. "None of my decorations survived the move."

"None of them?" Sherry gasped, shaking her head. "Oh, honey, I'm sorry. You must have been devastated."

Not even close. They were gone, and she was glad. She didn't want the reminder of Christmases she'd never have again and couldn't get back.

"You know, Sherry, whenever I think about what I've lost, I look at these adorable faces, and I count the three blessings I still have."

"Aaron would have loved them. He would have enjoyed all this." Sherry's face paled as she got choked up. "He should be here helping his dad get the tree. It all feels so wrong."

Nicole couldn't help surveying her pretty cabin, the babies in her arms and the stack of bakery items on the counter. While she sympathized with Sherry's grief, she'd done her best to pick up the pieces after Aaron had died. She was proud of how far she'd come. Her new life didn't feel wrong at all. In fact, it felt right.

Judd shoved his phone into his jacket pocket and started his truck. He'd called his mom earlier. He hadn't heard from his parents since finding out they'd bought the condo in Saint Thomas. After a brief conversation, she'd texted him several pictures of her and Dad laughing with a group of people at restaurants and the two of them hanging out on their new balcony. She'd even sent him a selfie on the beach.

Going on their merry way without a thought for him as usual. Feeling uncharacteristically lonely, he'd wanted to stop over at Nicole's, but her in-laws were there and he wouldn't intrude. So, he figured he'd do the next best thing. Stop in to visit Aunt Gretchen for a while.

As his truck rumbled down the drive

leading to the highway, he kept an eye out on his land. The cattle were thriving. He still needed to inspect one of his remote pastures soon. The weather forecast was calling for milder weather, which would save him on hay since the cows would be able to graze. No matter what, the stacks of bales in the hay yard should keep his herd fed throughout the winter.

He took a left onto the highway toward town. Up ahead, a mule deer carcass sat by the side of the road. He'd have to deal with it later. Roadkill attracted predators like coyotes, and he didn't want them anywhere near his cattle. Would the next person who owned his land protect it?

Why was estate planning so hard? He was tired of going round and round trying to make a decision.

Making a mental note to add moving the carcass to his list on the whiteboard in his ranch office, he turned on the radio. "The Christmas Song" played, and he pictured Nicole and the babies by a crackling fire. He could see himself there, too.

*I've got to stop thinking about her.*

The miles sped away until he reached town. Soon he parked behind a black truck in front of his aunt's one-story brick house and strode up the walkway. After he rapped a few quick knocks, she opened the door.

"Judd, what a nice surprise. Come in!" She held the storm door open for him, and he took off his outerwear, then followed her down the hall.

Instrumental Christmas music filled the air, and her house smelled like cinnamon and other spices. The essence of the holiday season. When he reached her living room, he stopped cold.

There in one of her chairs was… Stu Miller. What was he doing here?

"Howdy, Judd." Stu rose, the toothpick in his mouth bobbing, and came over to shake his hand.

Judd glanced at Aunt Gretchen to get an idea of what was going on. Maybe Stu had stopped by for something and she'd invited him to stay.

"I'll get a pot of coffee on." She beamed. "I made apple crumb cake earlier. Would you both like some?"

"I know I would." Stu grinned, watching her walk away with a wistful expression on his face.

"Count me in." Judd would just have to go with this, but the situation was bizarre. Aunt Gretchen never had men over that Judd knew of. Stu reclaimed the chair, and Judd sat on the couch. "What brings you over?"

Stu's cheeks flushed. "Last week your aunt and I were talking about how we both like to do jigsaw puzzles this time of year."

That was when Judd noticed a puzzle with part of the outline put together on the dining table adjacent to the living room.

"We got it started, and we're taking a break," Stu said. "These eyes don't see small pieces as good as they used to."

Aunt Gretchen bustled back in holding a tray filled with slices of cake, forks and napkins. She set the tray on the coffee table. "The coffee will be another minute."

She beamed at Stu, who smiled wider than the open sky.

Was Judd interrupting something? Like a date?

He'd never imagined Aunt Gretchen dating.

"I don't want to mess up your plans." Judd started to rise.

"What? No. Sit." She pointed to the couch. "I'll be right back with the coffee." She hurried back to the kitchen.

"You having any trouble with your pregnant cows?" Stu leaned forward, resting his elbows on his knees.

Judd wanted to be anywhere but here, but he'd make the best of it.

"No, they're good. These temps are helping."

"I always welcome a good thaw before winter comes to stay." Stu discussed the forecast, and Judd relaxed, chiming in with questions about his ranch.

Aunt Gretchen came back and poured

coffee for them all in mugs decorated with holly while Judd handed Stu a piece of cake.

"Okay, no more talking about cows, boys." She sat back and sipped her coffee. "We've got Christmas coming up. Stu, what are your plans for the day?"

"Church first thing." He sliced a fork into his piece of cake. "Dylan wants me to stop by Gabby's for a bit in the afternoon. I got little Phoebe a plastic shopping cart with play food and everything. She sure is a cutie."

"Phoebe will love it." She smiled. "Judd and I always have dinner at five. You should join us. Shouldn't he, Judd?" Her eyes were bright and sparkly. Judd couldn't remember the last time he'd seen her this happy.

His sweet aunt liked Stu Miller. Really liked him. And from the puppy-dog look on Stu's face, the feeling was more than mutual.

"Uh, of course," Judd stammered. "The more the merrier."

But his heart wasn't in it. What if Aunt Gretchen started to prefer Stu's company to his? Would she make Christmas plans without Judd from now on? Get tired of their nightly phone calls?

His parents didn't need him or want him around. Aunt Gretchen might get bored with him, too.

Things were changing. The crumb cake stuck to his throat.

He'd never been great with change. What if everyone moved forward without him?

He'd be alone.

He supposed he was used to it. But he wasn't sure he wanted to be a loner anymore.

"I don't know how you do it, Nicole." Sherry sat on Nicole's couch next to a laundry basket of freshly laundered baby clothes after church the next morning. She held up a sleeper with little basketballs all over it. "Getting the babies in and out of the church was a lot of work."

"It is, but I've got a system." Nicole reclined back in her favorite chair as she fed Amelia. Eli and Henry had already eaten, and Sherry had helped her put the boys down for a nap. Lance had noticed one of the strands of lights on the new tree had gone out, so he was fiddling with the bulbs and muttering about how nothing was made the way it used to be.

"Everyone certainly is helpful. I'll give you that." Stacks of clean folded baby clothes grew next to Sherry on the couch. "When the triplets get a little older, though, you won't have as much help."

"Why not?"

"You don't expect the ladies to come over in the mornings or hold a baby on their lap during church forever, do you?"

"Well, no, but..." Nicole hadn't thought too far into the future. She supposed the church ladies would stop coming over once the triplets were older. But how old? When they were walking? Sooner? Their first birthday was next summer. How would Nicole manage three toddlers on her own then?

"Lance and I have been talking." Sherry peeked at Lance. He'd found the faulty bulb. The tree now twinkled with various-colored lights. He wiped off his thighs and came over to stand next to his wife. She set a tiny pair of pink stretchy pants to the side and took her husband's hand in hers. "We think you should consider moving down to Oklahoma with us."

Oklahoma? Nicole flinched. Why? Did they have a problem with the way she was raising the babies?

"Our basement's finished. The grand-kids love playing down there." Lance smiled kindly. "There's a bedroom and bathroom. You'd have your own space."

Her own space? Her head was spinning. They didn't get it. Living in their base-ment was *not* having her own space.

She needed a kitchen.

She needed to bake.

Flashes of living with Mom and Stella made her stomach constrict. Being crammed into one bedroom with three babies and all their stuff had worn on her soul. Tiptoeing around a house that wasn't hers to avoid waking anyone and being bombarded with advice she didn't want or need had drained her.

She'd felt helpless.

Trapped.

"That's very kind of you." Her chest was so tight she could barely breathe. "I'm doing really well here, though."

"We would have offered sooner." Sherry studied the floor. "But we could tell you were set on moving in with your mother. It was a relief knowing she'd be helping you with the babies. But she's not around anymore, and it's not right that you have to rely on strangers to get by."

"They're retired women who dote on the triplets. They've all told me time and again how nice it is to spend time with the babies after years of not having any to hold."

"Oh, I'm sure they're all wonderful." Sherry snatched another onesie and folded it with military precision. "What if you get sick, though? Hurt? You're out here in the middle of nowhere with triplets. I'd feel much better if you were staying with us."

Nicole had worried about those things, too, but with Judd coming over on weeknights, she didn't fret about it anymore.

"Judd—" She almost told them he came over most weekdays. Saying it out loud would open herself up to their judgment, though, and they clearly hadn't been keen on the Judd subject yesterday. "Judd's right down the lane if I need anything. I can call him."

Amelia had fallen asleep in Nicole's arms and, needing a reprieve from the oppressive energy in the room, she took her down the hall and set her in the crib. Nicole could hear Lance and Sherry's hushed conversation, but she tuned it out.

She didn't want to move to Oklahoma. Couldn't imagine living in their basement.

This cabin, the churchwomen, Judd and her fledgling business had given her freedom. And, sure, relying on other people's generosity meant she wasn't standing on her own two feet, but in time she would be.

Living in Rendezvous was allowing her to build a foundation for a new life. One she wanted. One she could be proud of.

*Lord, I feel prickly right now, and I don't want to go out there and offend Aaron's parents. I know they're struggling with the loss of their son. And I know they mean well. They truly want to help. But I can't do it. If I move in with them, I'll have no freedom, no privacy and no means of supporting myself. How do I let them down easily?*

She cast one more look over the babies—they were all sleeping soundly—and returned to the living room.

"You don't have to make a decision today." Lance held up his hands. "Just think about it. And be practical. You're not working, and you wouldn't have to pay rent if you moved in with us. The life insurance policy will stretch further in Oklahoma."

The rent. Of course. They worried about her finances. Nicole decided to be honest with them.

"I worked out a barter arrangement with Judd about the rent." She was tired of hiding something that didn't need to be hidden. "I cook him supper four nights a week."

"I see." Sherry brushed nonexistent lint off her slacks.

Based on her mother-in-law's tone, Nicole doubted it.

"You told me you were concerned with how fast everything happened with your mom and her new boyfriend." Sherry's gaze felt like a laser beam. "And now they're living together far away. We don't want your circumstances to force you to follow in her footsteps."

Nicole's heart sliced open.

How could Sherry suggest such a thing? Didn't they believe in her at all?

If a time portal could open up right here,

right now, she would be forever grateful. Because standing in front of her former in-laws as they tried to convince her she was desperate and destined to become like her mother was certainly a new low point in her life.

"I would never be like my mother," she said quietly. Her mom's choices had affected her, mainly by convincing her she wouldn't settle for anything less than marriage. "I can only assume you're worried about my friendship with Judd, but you've never even met him and already assume the worst. He's a good man. A quiet rancher. He's God-fearing and generous. He's not preying on widows or whatever you're thinking. We're friends and have been ever since I moved back. He's also nothing like the men my mom, bless her heart, attracts. So feel free to think whatever you want about me but don't think poorly of him."

Lance looked taken aback, and Sherry paled.

"For the record, I am thankful for your

offer," Nicole said. "I know you want what's best for me and the triplets. I know you want to spend time with your grandchildren. It's very generous of you to offer me a place in your home. I want you to be part of the babies' lives. But I'm not moving anywhere." She tried to find the words to make them understand, but she wasn't sure she understood it herself. "This year…it's brought so many changes. I can't handle another change right now. I'm settled here. I'm getting my life together."

Sherry came over to her and took her hands in hers. "I'm sorry. I should have thought about my words more carefully before speaking them."

"I'm sorry, too." Lance joined them and slung his arm over Sherry's shoulders. "We're far away and don't always know what's going on. We shouldn't have assumed…"

"It's okay." Nicole tried to reassure them. "I understand. This is hard on all of us. You both have been so good to me my entire life. I…well… We'll get through this."

"Our offer still stands," Lance said. "If this arrangement in Rendezvous isn't working or you find you need more help, we'd love for you to come down. We'll always have a place for you."

"Thank you." She hugged him. "From the minute Aaron and I became friends all those years ago, you gave me much-needed stability. I love you both."

"We love you, too," they said in unison. They looked at each other and laughed.

"How about another slice of the carrot cake you made?" Lance said. "It sure hit the spot yesterday."

"Coming right up. Why don't you two find a Christmas movie for us?" Nicole went to the kitchen. She'd meant every word she'd said to them, but their judgment lingered. Why had they gotten a bad impression of her?

Their lack of faith in her hurt.

Nicole uncovered the two-tiered carrot cake with cream cheese frosting and cut three slices. The only things she'd done with Judd were sit in the same pew at church and walk around Christmas Fest. How anyone could assume the worst based on that was beyond her.

She'd tried so hard her entire life to be the exact opposite of her mom and sister. Clearly, it had been a waste of time. If only people could see she wasn't like them.

She and Judd were friends only. No one needed to know her feelings for him weren't purely platonic. But…if people around town were gossiping about them…

What if Judd had picked up on her attraction?

It would make him uncomfortable, and she couldn't bear the thought.

She'd better stop giving him mixed signals, or they'd both get hurt.

# *Chapter Eleven*

It had been a never-ending Monday on the ranch. As Judd had dealt with the broken fence a bull had destroyed, all he had been able to think about was how much he looked forward to coming over here. Three days without seeing Nicole or the triplets had felt like a lifetime. And now the reason for him to linger after supper was reaching its conclusion.

His aunt's gift was almost complete.

He and Nicole had finished eating a little while ago. Since then, he'd helped her get some of the walls assembled on the wooden base Stu had made. It was covered with parchment paper on the dining table. At this rate, they'd have most of the house together tonight.

"Hold these pieces steady while I attach the back." Nicole pointed to the three walls still standing upright.

Judd held them as Nicole piped royal icing around the edges of the gingerbread wall and stuck it into a thick band of icing she'd created to keep it in place. "I don't trust this will stay up. I'm going to grab a few glass jars. I'll be right back."

She disappeared into the kitchen while he kept the walls steady.

"How did the visit with your in-laws go?" he asked when she came back.

She kept her attention on placing the jars on either side of the wall so it wouldn't move. "It was okay."

Hmm... She was about as talkative as him. Unusual for her.

"How was your weekend?" she asked. "What did you end up doing?"

It had been an odd weekend for him. After hanging out with his aunt and Stu, he'd driven around, contemplating his future. The optimistic, unrealistic part of him could picture Nicole and the triplets here on the ranch forever.

But that wasn't going to happen.

So he'd driven past wide-open land and kept coming back to his conversation with Cash. Yesterday afternoon, he'd talked to Cash. Their chat had given him some clarity. Naming him as a beneficiary wasn't an ideal solution, but at least it was better than nothing.

"I paid Cash McCoy a visit yesterday." Judd had asked him if he'd ever considered owning a ranch other than the McCoys'. Cash grew serious, and a light had flashed in his eyes only to dim.

He'd said, "I was born to do this—take care of a herd, watch over the land. The McCoy property is in my blood. I hate what my brother is doing to it. Dad won't listen. We can't afford to keep paying off Chris's stupid debts. So yeah, if I had the opportunity to be the sole owner of another ranch, I'd take it. And I wouldn't waste it, either."

Judd knew sincerity when he heard it. And Cash had been sincere.

"Cash, huh?" Nicole bent to put a little more icing on a wall. "Are you close with him?"

"No." He shook his head. "I wouldn't say that. But their property isn't far from mine, and I wanted to discuss a few things."

"Like what?" Setting the bag of icing on the table, she selected the next section of gingerbread to attach.

"Like how he'd feel about running a ranch not owned by his family."

"That's a big question." She peered at him as she selected a small rectangle. "Why did you want to know?"

"I'm looking ahead. Planning my future." He enjoyed the way her mouth opened slightly as she lined icing on the top of the porch walls and stuck a small roof piece above them. "I have a few options now."

Two options, to be exact. One was what everyone kept telling him to do. *Get married. Have kids.* But he didn't see it happening. Just because he and Nicole got along okay making a gingerbread house didn't mean he could read more into it. Even if she hadn't lost her husband a year ago, she wouldn't seriously consider a future with Judd.

*I'm too quiet. Too old. Too reserved. Too...*

Women didn't want to spend forever with a guy like him.

"I'm assuming you're talking about your will. What are the options?" Nicole craned her neck to the side to check on the babies. They were making happy little noises in their bouncy seats. Every time Judd looked their way, something poked at his heart.

He wished things were different—wished *he* was different—so he could take everyone's advice and get married and have kids. Three for starters.

Was it so crazy?

"Everyone seems to think I should get married." He watched her closely, looking for the slightest indication she had feelings for him.

"What do you tell them?" She didn't bother looking up. The porch roof took all of her concentration.

"Nothing."

"You could, you know." She stared at him, and he spiraled into her green eyes.

He held his breath, wanting her to give him a sign, not knowing what it might be. His gaze had fallen to her pale pink lips, and he couldn't look away.

"What's the other option?" she asked.

Other option? What was she talking about?

Estate planning.

Right.

"I haven't made any decisions, but I think Cash would take care of the cattle and land the way I do."

"I didn't think you even liked him much."

"Usually, he's too slick."

"Yet you'd leave all of this to him?" She finished attaching the roof and stepped back, watching him.

"I don't know. The slick thing—I think it's an act. When it comes down to it, he's a rancher through and through."

Tilting her head, she studied the gingerbread house, then him.

"Why don't you want to get married, Judd?"

He froze, the delicate timbre of her voice echoing in his ears. He *did* want to get married. But he'd been rejected his whole life. He didn't have what it took to make a woman happy. His own parents didn't want to be around him. He couldn't bear to think he'd make Nicole miserable.

"I have nothing against marriage," he said gruffly. "If I found someone who accepted me the way I am, I might consider it."

Her face fell. Had he said the wrong thing? Probably.

"I know what you mean." She had a faraway look in her eyes. "I was friends with Aaron for so long—my entire life, really—before we got married. And we married young. I'm talking *young*." She arched her eyebrows. "After he was diagnosed with Becker muscular dystrophy, we both had this urgency to make the most of every minute together."

Judd hung on every word, although they soured in his stomach. How could he be falling for this woman, knowing she'd had the love of her life and lost him only a year ago? What kind of fool was he?

"The first couple of years were exciting. Aaron was going to college, and I got a job at the bakery. We had a tiny apartment off campus, and his health was the best it had been since before high school. We both believed he'd live to middle age and beyond. I learned so much at the bakery. I loved my job, even though it didn't pay well. After he graduated, he got hired on full-time with a company he'd interned for. I thought we'd start enjoying ourselves—going on all the dates we'd skipped because we didn't have the time or the money."

Her eyes clouded as if she was seeing her past.

"But instead of growing closer, we'd been slowly growing apart. I thought it was fixable. I thought having children would unite us."

"They would have." He tried to reassure her. "Look at these three. Your husband would have loved them."

Her throat worked as she nodded. "He would have loved them. I know that's true. But our marriage? I'm not trying to knock Aaron, but his college experience shifted the way he looked at me. He respected the intelligent, ambitious women he worked with. He'd hint that I should go to college. He didn't understand why I was content working at a bakery. I wasn't good enough for him anymore."

A rush of protectiveness brought with it a few choice words for her husband. Wanting to tell off a dead guy who couldn't defend himself? Ridiculous.

"People are stupid sometimes." His voice was gruff. "You have a talent for baking, and you should never waste the gifts God gave you."

A smile spread across her face, lighting her eyes. "That's one of the nicest things anyone's ever said to me. Thank you."

"Yeah, well, I mean it." Her joyful face was giving him visions of roses and first dates. He needed to get his thoughts back to neutral. "I wouldn't change a thing about you."

Her cheeks flushed as she looked away. "Why do you think a woman wouldn't accept you?"

His neck grew warm. It was good and all to listen to Nicole talk about her husband, but he didn't think it would be wise to share his past with her. What if she agreed with his exes?

Shouldn't he at least give her the benefit of the doubt?

"I'm not much of a talker." He clenched and unclenched his jaw. "Not open with my feelings."

"I imagine the right woman would be able to read between the lines." Understanding shimmered in her eyes. "Not all of us want every minute to be filled with conversation."

Her words gave him hope, and with the way her eyes were dancing, he'd like nothing more than to round the table and stare down into them. Take her in his arms and touch her golden hair. Let her read between the lines by kissing her—showing her how deep his feelings went.

"Aaron talked all the time." A wistful smile lifted her lips. "I was out of the house by the time he woke, but as soon as he got home, he'd tell me all about his day and the people he worked with and the projects he wanted and the promotion he hoped to get. Talk, talk, talk. I didn't mind. I liked hearing about his day."

Great. Another reminder he was nothing like her husband.

"But he never asked about mine," she said so quietly he almost missed it. She picked up another wall. "That's one of the things I like about you. You care about what other people are doing. You're comfortable enough in your own skin to not fill every minute with words."

Every syllable broke down the barriers around his heart.

She seemed to admire the very thing that drove women away from him.

In that moment, he realized he loved her. He loved Nicole Taylor.

Grinding his teeth together, he tried to get a grip on the topsy-turvy feeling in his heart.

He'd been given a precious gift. The gift of being accepted unconditionally.

Unfortunately, acceptance from Nicole would never be enough.

He loved her. And he'd always want her to love him back.

Why was Judd so quiet all of a sudden? She hoped he didn't think less of her for telling the truth about Aaron.

Well, if he did, she couldn't help it. Talking candidly with him had been exactly what she needed. After the awkward weekend with her in-laws, she'd fretted about the things she'd said to them, too. Had she defended Judd too much? Had they read into it and seen the truth? That she really cared about this guy?

It was wrong—so wrong—to have these feelings. But how could she not be drawn to the man?

His quiet strength had gotten her through many social functions she hadn't wanted to attend this year. She'd only gone to them because her mom had forced her to and because she was afraid of falling into a depression she'd never be able to climb out of. But she'd also known she could sit with Judd. He made no demands from her. Just welcomed her. What a gift.

On top of that, he'd offered her this cabin. Refused to accept rent. And moments ago, he'd told her she had a talent for baking and that she shouldn't waste her gifts.

He was so beyond her definition of the perfect guy it wasn't even funny.

The thing about Judd? He always acted as if *she* impressed him.

She'd never—ever—impressed anyone besides her old boss.

Not Aaron. Not her mother.

No one.

That was why she needed to be careful about his feelings. He was private. A loner. Not interested in marriage.

"I hate to bring this up," she said. "But I think people are talking about us around town."

"Talking about us. What do you mean?" His face held a tinge of green. Exactly as she'd feared. He must hate the idea of people mentally pairing them together.

The way he'd been looking at her and the things they'd been sharing tonight had sprinkled hope inside her that he might feel more for her, too.

Apparently not.

"My in-laws are concerned. Their friends said something to them."

"They have nothing to be concerned about," he snapped. "People are always sticking their noses in things they shouldn't."

"I told them you were honorable and kind and they shouldn't jump to conclusions." She kept her attention on the royal icing, her heart sinking at his reaction. Was he disgusted at the thought of people linking them romantically?

"I'm sorry, Nicole." His cheeks puffed as he exhaled. "I should have known people would talk. It's not fair to you."

"I don't care. Let them talk." She attached another piece, holding it until she was sure it would stand on its own. "We haven't done anything wrong."

But could she truly say that? Her feelings toward Judd might not be wrong, but they didn't seem right, either.

"I don't have to drive you to church anymore." He didn't sound happy, and two lines grooved in his forehead.

"I like going to church together." She didn't want to drive separately. "I mean, I can handle driving the triplets and all, but it seems like a waste of gas for us to take two vehicles."

"It is a waste."

"I'm not worried about a little gossip. I've got enough to deal with trying to take care of these babies every day." As if to punctuate the thought, Amelia let out a few whimpers.

"Exactly."

"Don't get me wrong—I'm not complaining," she added quickly. "I can handle them. In fact, Sherry and Lance kind of made me mad this weekend by suggesting otherwise."

"What do you mean?" He'd moved around the table and bent to give Amelia her pacifier. When he rose, he stood mere inches from Nicole.

He smelled spicy and woodsy. Her nerves were ping-ponging all over the place.

She should shift to give him more room. But she didn't.

She supposed flippy nerves were a welcome change from the grief, depression and exhaustion she'd dealt with for so long. In fact, standing next to Judd Wilson brought all the good feels her life had been missing.

"My in-laws want me to move to Oklahoma." The words flew out. "To live in their basement. Apparently, they're worried about me out here on the ranch, and they think everyone will get tired of helping me out. I told them I was fine, and if anything happened, I could call you, but they weren't convinced."

"You can call me. Anytime. I'll be here." The low words fired warmth in her core. "And everyone wants to help you out."

"I know." She could barely think straight with him so close. "They weren't real happy about it, of course, but their hearts were in the right place. It was kind of them to offer."

"So you're not going?"

"No." His blue eyes drew her in, making her pulse beat faster. "My life is finally starting to make sense here."

"Good. I..." He hesitated, running his

fingers through his hair. "I want you to do whatever's best for you."

His words deflated some of her nervous energy. "Well, living in their basement would not be what's best for me. Once again, I'd be sharing a room with three babies. And I can't imagine not having my own kitchen again. Baking has given me a piece of myself back. I probably sound ungrateful."

"You don't."

The bag of icing dropped out of her hand. They both reached down to pick it up.

As she rose, she couldn't drag her eyes away from his mouth. She was acutely aware of his gaze falling to her lips. Of her foot taking a step closer to him. Of his sharp intake of breath.

Of his big, strong hands gently clasping her waist.

Of her own hands tentatively reaching up behind his neck, touching his soft dark hair.

Then his lips pressed against hers, and the sensation was all new.

Just like the man himself, his kiss was gentle, firm and generous.

He didn't take. He gave. And tasting the cinnamon on his lips pushed her closer to him as she kissed him back. As he tightened his hold on her, sensations flooded her mind until they sharpened. She needed this connection. Wanted his acceptance. Savored his touch.

Too soon, he ended the kiss. Excitement and a hint of fear lingered in his eyes. Then he took two steps backward, almost tripping over a bouncy seat. His face grew red.

"I'm sorry, Nicole. I don't know what came over me." With a few long strides, he grabbed his coat and fled out the door.

At the click of it shutting, reality fell like concrete blocks on her shoulders.

One year ago, she'd been pleading with God for Aaron's life.

And tonight, she'd kissed another man and liked it.

More than liked it.

She wanted more.

She'd never been kissed like that.

Maybe she was just like her mother after all.

# *Chapter Twelve*

Of all the stupid things he could have done, kissing Nicole topped the list. Judd braced himself against the stinging snow as he rode out to check cows the following afternoon. Not wanting Aunt Gretchen to see the gingerbread house when she came to help out with the babies, he'd gone to Nicole's first thing this morning, mumbled hello, avoided looking her in the eye and carefully balanced the house all the way to his truck. He'd managed to carry it into his kitchen without incident. Shocking, considering how shaky his hands had been.

He'd have to apologize tonight at supper. Losing Nicole's friendship wasn't a scenario he cared to contemplate.

He needed her too much.

Up ahead, two black cows huddled together. Every now and then, they'd lower their necks and chomp on the weeds and grass. They barely noticed as he pulled up alongside them. Seeing nothing out of the ordinary, he pressed forward.

His cell phone rang. He tugged it out of his coat pocket. Aunt Gretchen. Was something wrong? She never called at this time. Taking off his leather glove, he swiped the phone.

"What's going on?" he asked.

"Sorry to bother you, Judd, but I need a favor. I asked Nicole to come to our Christmas dinner. I don't think she has plans, but she didn't accept my invitation, either. I don't want her to be alone on Christmas. I was wondering if you'd invite her, too."

After kissing Nicole, he wouldn't mind spending every holiday, evening, morning and in between with her, but he wasn't telling Aunt Gretch any of that.

"It's going to be a hard day for her," he said. The cold almost made him lose his grip on the phone. "She might not want to be around anyone. The first anniversary of her husband's death won't be easy."

"Which is precisely why I want her to come over. She needs support. Her mother won't be around, and I doubt Stella will come home, either."

He didn't want Nicole thinking he was pressuring her on account of their kiss. She had too much stress in her life to think about dating. And it was probably too soon after losing her husband, anyhow. If he asked her to join him at Aunt Gretchen's for Christmas, she might read more into it than she should.

"Judd? Are you there?"

"Yes."

"Will you ask her? For me?"

He'd never been able to tell his aunt no, but asking Nicole was sure to be awkward. He let out a heavy sigh. "Yes."

"Thank you! I'll let you go. Oh, Stu is picking me up on Thursday for the Christmas Eve service. We'll save you a spot."

He said goodbye and hung up, resuming his inspection of the cattle. Since when did Aunt Gretchen sit with Stu Miller on Christmas Eve?

He supposed it was time to accept the fact she'd found someone who made her happy. Stu doted on her. It kind of stank that Judd's seventy-year-old aunt had a better dating life than he did.

Dallas approached on horseback. "They all checked out."

"Good. Let's head back." The wind had calmed down and, as they made their way across the plain, the snow subsided, making it more pleasant to ride. The quiet of winter cleared his head. All the reasons he shouldn't be with Nicole rushed into his mind.

He was too quiet.

But...she'd told him she liked being with him because he didn't fill every minute with words.

Well, then there was the fact she was a grieving widow.

But…she seemed to be moving forward, and her marriage hadn't been perfect the way he'd thought.

She had three babies.

But…he loved all three of those babies, and she seemed to appreciate his help with them.

There was no denying he was too old for her.

But… Nicole teased him about it, but she was just being nice.

He was too old for her, wasn't he?

"How old is too old to date someone?" Judd glanced over at Dallas.

"What do you mean?" The cowboy looked confused. "Are we talking about old people? Or teenagers?"

"Like me." He barely choked out the words.

"Yeah, you've got one foot in the grave, old man." Dallas grinned.

"I'm being serious." He should have

known Dallas would take it the wrong way. This was why he didn't ask for advice.

"Depends on who it is." Dallas shrugged. "Yes, you're too old to date a sophomore in high school. No, you're not too old to date a grown woman."

"I would never even look at a high school girl."

"I know." He laughed. "That's why it's fun to say it. Who do you have your eye on? Misty? Eden? The new receptionist at the inn?"

"No one." Only the most beautiful woman with long blond hair and sage-green eyes who baked the most delicious concoctions and was the sweetest mother he'd ever known.

"It's got to be someone I know," Dallas said.

"Forget I said anything."

"It can't be Nicole."

Terrific, even Dallas knew Nicole was off-limits. Why couldn't Judd's heart take the hint?

"I mean, she's hot and all, but three kids? Ick. No guy wants to take on three babies." Dallas grimaced.

Judd was taken aback. Although the air was frigid, his body grew toasty warm. Dallas had discounted Nicole on account of the triplets. Not because of Judd's age.

"Thanks, Dallas." He felt positively cheerful.

"For what?"

"For being you."

Judd rode taller in the saddle. Maybe he didn't need to apologize to Nicole for kissing her. He was a grown man. She was a mature woman. They were both single. They were comfortable in each other's company.

He would invite her to Aunt Gretchen's Christmas dinner. Whether she accepted or not wasn't up to him.

And it was high time he bought presents for her and the babies.

The perfect Christmas gift for Nicole

came to mind. He'd go into town tomorrow. She was going to love it.

And if everyone talked after he gave it to her, so be it.

Nicole propped Henry on her hip and attempted to finish making mint-green Christmas trees out of gum paste to decorate the yard. Judd would be back with the gingerbread house any minute. She tried to keep her focus on what still needed to be done, but her mind kept going back to his kiss last night.

It had felt so right.

And it had been so wrong.

Earlier, Gretchen had invited her to join them at Christmas dinner. Nicole had declined. She'd jumped into feelings too soon. One year wasn't long enough. She'd been wrong to encourage Judd and send him mixed signals. From now on, she was going to be the tenant she should have been all along. Friendly. With boundaries.

The envelope next to her stack of mail drew her gaze. She'd saved all the money she'd earned from the holiday baking. Just thinking about the small sum filled her with courage. It wasn't much, but she'd earned every penny.

Henry reached out to touch one of the trees, and she gently pulled his chubby fingers back. "Uh-uh, these aren't for you, Mr. Monkey." He let out a frustrated squawk, and she knew how he felt.

She'd never get the decorations finished at this rate. She still needed to attach the top roof and put all the disc candies on it for shingles.

Part of her wanted the decorating to last. And part of her wanted to wrap it up as soon as possible. Spending less time with Judd was going to take some getting used to. Every hour together only drew her closer to him.

It wasn't fair to either of them.

She didn't know if what she felt was real or a natural effect of being lonely. Her lack of experience with the opposite sex didn't help matters.

All she knew was a year wasn't enough

to get over her best friend. It was one thing to move forward by not thinking about Aaron constantly, and it was an entirely other thing to give her heart to another man.

For the first time, she sympathized with her mom. She'd never truly understood how her mother could flip from normal to giddy-schoolgirl-with-a-crush in three seconds flat.

Maybe she'd been too hard on Mom over the years.

*I don't have to be like her. I have choices. And the wise choice is to freeze these feelings for Judd.*

Two knocks on the door almost made her jump.

"It's unlocked. Come in," she called. Her heartbeat pounded out *pa rum pum pum pum* as Judd entered.

"Can you hold the door open for me?" he asked. "I'll bring the house back inside."

"Sure." She hustled over to the door, shielding Henry from the blast of cold, as Judd hauled the gingerbread house inside and onto the table.

Amelia made cooing noises as soon as she heard Judd's voice. He hung up his coat and rubbed his palms together before making his way over to her. Then he crouched in front of the seat. She kicked her pajama-covered legs in delight. The sight caused the bottom of Nicole's heart to fall out. This man was so good with her babies. He was good to her, too.

"How are you, little sweet pea?" He tickled the bottoms of her feet and she squealed in delight. "You're awfully happy tonight. Did Mommy give you a treat or something?" He unstrapped her and lifted her into his arms.

"No treats. She just likes you. I made a light supper so we could finish this up."

His face fell. "What do you want me to do?"

"Let's eat first." She tweaked Henry's nose and he opened his mouth in a smile. "I've got to set this little guy down. Help yourself to a sloppy joe. They're on the stove."

After getting Henry settled, she fixed herself a plate and joined Judd at the table. "So what did you do today?"

She probably shouldn't be asking him about his day, but she loved hearing what he did on the ranch. It was so foreign to her indoor life.

He still held Amelia in one arm as he ate. "Checked fence. Fed cows. Made sure our pregnant gals are doing okay. The usual."

"Think the snow will come back tonight?"

"I don't think so. It's supposed to be real cold, though." He met her eyes and her mouth went dry. He was so handsome. "What about your day? Did you finish the pies for the Seymours?"

How could she put distance between them when he actually asked about her day and seemed to care?

"I did. Rodney picked them up this afternoon. I have two yule logs to make tomorrow and I'll be done until New Year's."

"How did the new flavors go for the pie? Did you try the apple and cranberry?"

"I did. I added a brown sugar crumble to make sure it wasn't too tart."

His eyes gleamed with appreciation as he nodded. They continued eating in silence, and she couldn't help looking ahead and missing these times. But putting an end to this had to be done.

She knew it was necessary. It didn't mean she had to like it.

"All we have to do is attach the roof. Then we'll be able to add all the front yard decorations." If she kept her focus on the house, she could avoid dealing with the pain in her heart. "I bought wafer candies for the roof shingles. We'll have to wait until the roof is set to put them on, though."

"You've thought of everything. I don't know how I could ever repay you."

"You already have." And she meant

it. He owed her nothing. And she owed him…so much.

"What are you doing Christmas Day?" he asked.

She couldn't think about it. Couldn't make plans. All she knew was she'd dreaded it for 364 days, and if she got to December 26 without completely falling apart, she'd be okay.

"Aunt Gretchen is having a small dinner," he said. "You should come."

She wanted to. It would be nice to be with Judd and his aunt at her cute little house in town. No thoughts about Aaron or ICUs or dreaded doctors or the final moments she'd rebelled against with every fiber in her being.

"I don't think so." Grabbing her napkin, she covered her lips and tried to get her emotions under control. When she was reasonably sure she'd pushed away the pain, she looked up. Judd watched her intently.

"Is this about last night?" he asked. "I

didn't mean… I should have… I… Well, I don't know what to say."

Was he trying to apologize for kissing her? She almost started laughing. Maybe she was losing it or something. From pending tears to the uncontrollable urge to cackle in a split second.

"It's not about last night, Judd." She actually sounded composed. "Maybe a little. I don't know. I don't want to talk about it. Let's just enjoy finishing the house."

He blinked in surprise. She didn't want to hurt him. She also didn't want to discuss it when her insides were such a whirlwind.

Suppers together had been the best thing she had going, and she could finally admit it—she needed them to end.

Before she made a fool of herself.

She wasn't in a position to give him what he wanted. She was a widow with three babies, and she owed her dead husband the honor of waiting a respectable time before attempting a new relationship.

After tomorrow night, the gingerbread

house would be finished. The following day was Christmas Eve. She'd wait until then to have a heart-to-heart with Judd. And she'd try to enjoy what time she had left with him until then. As friends.

Judd shifted the shopping bags to his left hand and opened the door to Cattle Drive Coffee. He'd picked up Christmas presents for the triplets—stuffed horses and three T-shirts that each said Ho. He chuckled thinking of the babies lined up with shirts saying Ho, Ho, Ho. He also found a pink apron with Bakers Gotta Bake written on it for Nicole. He had one more stop to make before heading back to the ranch and helping Nicole put the final touches on the gingerbread house, but first, he needed a strong cup of coffee.

Nicole's cryptic words last night when he'd made the lame attempt at an apology for kissing her had been circling his brain.

He shouldn't have kissed her. It jeopardized their friendship. He could feel her putting on the brakes.

"Can I help you?" A teenage girl stood behind the counter.

"I'll take a black coffee to go."

Maybe he was reading too much into it. Maybe Nicole was just struggling with memories from last year.

The bell above the door clanged. He paid the girl, accepted the cup from her and turned to leave. Ryder Fanning, Mason's identical twin, was flanked by his twin four-year-old daughters.

"Can I get hot chocolate, Daddy?" One of the girls lifted big eyes to Ryder.

"I want some, too!"

"With whipped cream?" Ryder smiled at each of them.

"And marshmallows!" they said in unison.

"We're on Christmas vacation." Ryder chuckled. "You can get whatever you want."

Judd walked forward and nodded to him. "Ryder."

"Oh, hey, Judd. How are you doing?"

"Good. I didn't know you were coming into town."

"Yeah, we're staying with Mason and Brittany."

"We're going to make a snowman with Noah!" One of the girls jumped up, clapping her hands.

Noah was Mason's four-year-old son. Judd smiled at both the girls. "Sounds like a lot of fun."

"Last year we made a big fort." The other twin spread her arms wide. "We're going to make another one, right, Daddy?"

"I don't see why not." Ryder pushed them forward. "Why don't you two pick out your cookies while I catch up with Judd a minute?"

They raced to the front counter.

"How long are you in town for?" Judd asked.

"Until the third of January. But next year...well, I've been thinking about moving here permanently."

"Oh, yeah?"

"I want to get the girls out of the city.

Let them run around on a big old ranch the way I did growing up. I've been talking to Mason about it, and I might have found the opportunity I've been searching for."

"Would you work with him?" Judd wouldn't be surprised if Mason partnered up with his twin brother.

"No. He has his own land, and I want my own, too." Ryder stared off into space with a gleam in his eyes and a soft smile on his lips. "It's up in the air at the moment, but I'm hoping the girls and I will be residents of Rendezvous come spring. What are you up to? Looks like you're getting in some last-minute shopping." He hitched his chin to the bags in Judd's hands.

"That's exactly what I'm doing."

"Daddy, can we get the big chocolate chip cookies?" The twins ran back over to them, tugging on Ryder's arm. "When do we get to see Auntie Eden?"

Ryder frowned. "Yes, you can get the cookies."

"Can Auntie Eden come over tonight?"

"No." His sharp tone surprised Judd. "She has her own life, girls."

"Well, I won't keep you." Judd nodded to him.

"I'm sure I'll see you soon." Ryder followed the girls to the counter.

Judd opened the door and stepped onto the sidewalk. In a few short years the triplets would be begging for big cookies and bouncing off the walls about making a fort and a snowman. He wouldn't mind if they dragged him to the counter.

He wouldn't mind if they called him Daddy.

Frowning, Judd strolled to the last store on his list. He was getting Nicole a special gift. Whatever she felt for him didn't matter. He wanted her to have something meaningful, and he knew exactly what to get her. Maybe in time she'd be ready for a relationship with him. He'd just have to be patient.

# *Chapter Thirteen*

Christmas Eve had arrived, and Nicole bristled with pent-up tension. She pushed the curtain back from the living room window to check if Judd was on his way. No sign of him yet. She'd asked him to stop by when he finished his ranch chores. He'd told her he'd stop by at two. The babies were napping. So far, Christmas Eve had been like most other days, except without any outside help. Thoughts of Aaron and last Christmas kept assaulting her, and she, in turn, kept pushing them away.

Her nerves had been frazzled all day.

What she was about to do was going to break her heart. It was going to break Judd's, too. She couldn't pretend these feelings weren't mutual. Not after his kiss on Monday.

Last night had been bittersweet, she and Judd treading lightly while working together to finish his aunt's gift. He'd helped attach the pink wafer candies to the roof. They'd also lined a sidewalk path to the gingerbread house with small marshmallows and added a yard made out of white frosting. Green Christmas trees and pink candies completed the scene. The gingerbread house was an enchanting replica of Gretchen's childhood home. Judd had taken it back to his house when they finished.

A knock on the door made her jump. Her pulse went from zero to sixty in two seconds flat. Nicole made her way to the door, dreading every step. This wasn't how she wanted Christmas Eve to go down. Last year had been horrendous. This year wouldn't be much better.

After smoothing her sweater, she pulled her shoulders back and opened the door.

Judd's jacket was open. He had a Stetson on his head, a dark T-shirt stretched across his chest, and jeans skimmed his hips. His eyes drew her in, made her want to chuck her dumb plan and wrap her arms around him instead.

He took off his hat as he entered. "Merry Christmas Eve."

"Same to you." Her voice sounded too high, too bright. The way Judd was looking at her made her face warm. "Thanks for coming over."

"Where are the babies?" He took a seat on the couch, his knees wide, as he looked around.

"Napping." She went to the kitchen and took a deep breath, then carried the box of cupcakes she'd made him to the living room and set them on the end table. Then she selected a wrapped box from under the tree and brought it over to him. "I wanted to give you your present."

"You didn't have to get me anything."

His lips curved into a surprised smile at the sight of the shiny red wrapping paper.

"Yes, I did. I wanted to. You've done so much for me."

"That's what friends are for," he said seriously.

Friends. Turning away, she winced. He'd been the friend she'd needed for a long time. But her feelings kept tipping past the friend point. And now…

This wasn't going to end well.

"Go ahead and open it." She sat kitty-corner from him, keenly aware of the envelope she'd slipped into her pocket. He loosened the side flaps of the paper and carefully unwrapped the box. A quick glance her way made her feel even guiltier as he lifted the top off it. Then he pulled out the soft wool blanket she'd ordered.

"Wow, this is nice." He held it up, and it almost hurt to see the gratitude shining in his expression.

She gestured to the box on the end table. "I have a box of cupcakes for you, too. Death by chocolate."

"You baked for me?" His smile grew even broader. "Thank you."

The envelope in her pocket burned against her leg. *You have to give it to him. You know you do.*

She tugged it out, reached over and handed it to him before her mushy heart convinced her not to. "This is for you, too."

"What is it?" His forehead furrowed. He opened it, and his frown deepened. "I don't understand."

"I'm earning an income now." She held herself stiffly with her hands in her lap. "I want to pay you rent."

"Rent?" He shook his head. "I told you I don't want your money." He closed the envelope, pushing it away from him.

"But I want you to have it." Her voice rose. "I need to pay my own way."

"What's this about?" He shook his head. "Save your money. You need it more than I do."

"It's not about that." She squirmed, keeping her attention on her hands in her lap. "I've enjoyed spending time with you, Judd." No truer words had been spoken. "But the gingerbread house is finished, and I..."

Understanding dawned as his expression darkened. "You don't want me coming around for supper anymore."

She didn't know how to reply, so she sat there silently.

"Am I just a landlord to you?" The color in his face drained.

"No, of course not, but this—" she waved her hand between him and her "—is going too fast."

"I know. I'm sorry. We can slow it down..."

"No, we can't." She jumped to her feet and crossed over to the fireplace mantel. How could she make him understand? She whirled to face him. "*I* can't. I can't do this."

"You can't do what? Be happy?" He rose and joined her. She wanted to push him away, but he stood before her, and even now his arms beckoned. She craved his embrace.

"Like my mom, right?" she said. "All she cares about is being happy."

"What's wrong with being happy?" He caressed her cheek with the back of his hand. It shattered her. All the emotions and memories she'd been holding at bay crashed down.

"I can't be happy. It's not right!" The past and present collided in her brain. Last Christmas. This Christmas. What was happening?

"Nicole—"

"I'm not like everyone else. One year ago I was hunched in a chair next to my husband's bed in the hospital." Nicole wiped her palms down her cheeks. "I thought my life was over. I couldn't see a future without Aaron in it."

"I'm sorry—"

"Let me finish." She held up a hand. "He was hooked up to machines. His cheeks were drawn. Eye sockets sunken. I knew he wasn't going to make it, but I still begged God—begged Him—to let Aaron live."

She could see it all. Her sad little self in black leggings and a long sweater. Hair unwashed, pulled behind her in a ponytail. She'd never felt so small, so alone in her life.

"His parents and sisters and I stood by his bed telling him how much we loved him. I stayed there after they went back to their hotel. His hand was in mine, and I talked to him until I fell asleep in the chair. I woke up on Christmas morning, and I thought he was sleeping, but he wasn't. He'd passed away in the night. I thought my tears would never stop falling."

The weight of it all crushed her. The smell of the hospital was in her nostrils, the sound of the machines and Aaron's labored breathing were in her ears.

The fireplace mantel dug into her upper back, bringing her to the present.

"I loved him, Judd." She looked into

his blue eyes as her own misted. “He was there, and then he was gone.”

Tears ran down her cheeks, and her body began to tremble.

“He never came home, Judd.” She covered her face with her hands. “He never came home.”

Judd sprang into action as Nicole’s knees buckled. He swept her into his arms and carried her to the couch, keeping her close to him. She buried her face into his chest. Heartbreaking sobs racked her body. He’d never felt this helpless in his life.

The slap of pain he’d felt when she told him she was paying him rent to let him know she didn’t want to spend time with him anymore was nothing compared to this.

For the first time, he fully understood why he couldn’t have Nicole.

She belonged to someone else.

He stroked her hair as she cried, wanting to comfort her any way he could. Her fists balled into his shirt, and the material grew wet with her tears. He held her closer, wishing he could take away all her pain.

Why had he fallen in love with her? Why couldn't he have fallen for someone who would actually love him back?

Her sobs began to subside, but she didn't move away from him. Her fingers gripped his shirt.

"I'm sorry." Her voice was the faintest of whispers.

"Don't be." He caressed her hair even as it ripped his heart open, knowing he'd never hold her again.

This was the last time he'd give his heart away.

It wasn't his to give any longer.

It was hers. It would always be hers.

Soon, he'd slink back to his big house. Heat up frozen meals and eat his supper alone. He wanted to tell her she'd given him the best month of his life, but he wouldn't. He'd never tell her the truth.

The presents he'd wrapped for her and the babies were back home under his

Christmas tree. He'd been planning on bringing them over tomorrow. He still wanted her to have them. Maybe he'd just leave them on her doorstep. It would be less awkward that way.

He kept touching her hair, trying not to think about how depressing life was going to be without her friendship.

Kissing her the other night had been his biggest mistake. He never should have done it. If he hadn't, they might still be friends. She wouldn't have banished him. Wouldn't have felt the need to give him rent and cut off their evenings together.

Part of him knew it was always going to end like this. He'd just assumed he'd be the reason it ended. He'd never thought a dead man would be to blame.

Time slipped away as they sat there until a whimper from the babies' room caught his attention. He glanced down at Nicole, surprised to see she'd fallen asleep. Carefully, he shifted her to lie on the couch with a throw pillow under her head. Then he wriggled to stand. He covered her with a blanket and went to check on the babies.

Amelia grabbed her feet and smiled when he stood over her crib.

"Hey there, little lady." He picked her up, cradling her to his chest and kissing her forehead. "You look like you're raring to go."

He continued talking to her as he changed her diaper. The boys began to wake up. One by one, he changed them, too, then took each out and settled them in their bouncy seats in the living room. Nicole was sleeping on the couch.

The babies seemed fussy, so he warmed up three bottles he found in the fridge. Sitting on the floor, he fed the boys the way he'd seen Nicole do it.

The afternoon passed and the sky grew dark outside the windows. He took care of the babies until Nicole stirred. She pressed her palm to the side of her head as she sat up. Then she squinted as she took in Judd with the babies.

"What are you doing here? What time is it?"

"I'm just leaving. It's about five thirty." He crossed the room, pulled his jacket from the hook on the wall and shoved his arms into it. Grabbed the box with the blanket she'd given him. Left the envelope with the rent on the coffee table. "They've all been fed and changed."

He firmed his shoulders and strode to the front door. She didn't want him around anymore. He'd respect her wishes.

But before he left, he turned back to her. "If you need anything... Well, I'm probably the last person you'd call, so it doesn't matter." Her lips parted as his words hit home. "Merry Christmas, Nicole. I won't bother you again."

He slipped outside, closing the door behind him. He tucked the box under his armpit and headed down the lane home. Snowflakes were falling. The big fat ones. His favorite kind. He pulled his jacket closer to his body as the cold seeped in.

Halfway home, his steps faltered. The night was cold. But his heart was colder. He doubted it would ever thaw out again.

# Chapter Fourteen

How had her life gone so wrong?

As Christmas Eve ticked away, Nicole flipped through the channels. She sat on the floor with the babies snuggled up on the quilted mat next to her. She'd skipped supper. She'd missed church. Ever since Judd left, she'd been in a daze.

A commercial with a soldier on the doorstep and a woman crying came on. Flip. People laughing at a holiday party. Flip. A horror movie. Why would a horror movie be playing on Christmas Eve? She turned the television off.

Her life had become a horror movie

in the span of a few hours. Yes, she was being dramatic, but really, what was there to look forward to anymore?

She'd hurt Judd terribly.

She'd fallen apart over Aaron's death.

She'd passed out while Judd took care of the babies. Her babies. After she'd treated him so poorly. It was a wonder he hadn't sprinted out of here as soon as she'd given him the envelope with the rent money.

Her gaze fell to the coffee table, where the envelope taunted her. She didn't have the energy to see if he'd taken the box of cupcakes she'd made him. At least the wool blanket she'd given him was gone.

He'd probably tossed it in the trash. Along with what was left of her heart.

Her eyes welled with tears, and her lips wobbled as she regarded the babies.

Henry yawned. His lips smacked as he cuddled closer to her. Eli was almost asleep next to him. Amelia's mouth had formed an O, her little arms up by her ears as she slept.

"I'll get you to bed, dear ones."

She stood and carried each baby to their cribs. After blowing them a kiss from the doorway, she went back to the living room and curled up on the couch.

Now what? Christmas Eve had been a disaster. Judd was never going to speak to her again. Tomorrow was the anniversary of the worst day of her life. And to top it all off, she was alone.

Maybe she *should* move to Oklahoma. The triplets would be with their grandparents. She'd have lots of help. She wouldn't have to worry about developing inappropriate feelings for anyone.

It had been stupid to ask Judd if she could live in this cabin. Even then she'd been drawn to him. Even then she'd known she was attracted to him.

And she'd done it anyway.

*Like mother, like daughter.*

Closing her eyes, she shook her head and prayed. *God, I'm sorry. I'm an awful person. I'm no better than my mom. I don't know how to fix this. I don't know what I'm doing.*

Guilt spun like a tornado in her core. *I'm a judgy daughter. A terrible daughter-in-law. A selfish friend.*

A knock on the door interrupted her thoughts.

Her heart flooded with hope. Could it be Judd?

She scampered to her feet and opened the door. Eden stood on her porch.

"I didn't see you at church and I texted a few times. When I didn't hear from you, I got worried. I hope it's okay I stopped by."

"Oh, Eden." Nicole pulled her inside. "You have no idea how much I needed you. I've made a mess of everything..."

"Go. Change into your pajamas. I'm making us some decaf." Eden shooed her down the hall.

With shaking hands, Nicole changed into fuzzy pj's. *Thank You, God, for sending Eden.* Her presence was like the glow of a lamp in a dark cave.

"Is it okay if we have some of this pie?" Eden called.

"Yes." She hurried down the hallway

and to the kitchen. Eden had two slices of pumpkin pie topped with mounds of whipped cream in her hands.

"Come on. We'll eat in the living room." Eden tilted her head for Nicole to join her.

"I'll bring the coffee." The coffee maker's grumble told Nicole it was almost ready. She pulled two mugs out of the cupboard and poured flavored cream into them before filling them with coffee. Then she brought the mugs to the living room and set one in front of Eden and kept the other in her hands as she settled on the couch.

"Rough day, huh?" Eden's eyes glistened with sympathy.

"Yeah." Great, she was getting choked up. Again. "It's been awful."

"I can imagine. A lot of bad memories from last year to deal with."

"Too many." She sipped her coffee. All the guilt on her chest made it hard to breathe. She desperately needed to get some of it off before it consumed her. "I'm dealing with a lot of new stuff this year, too. The memories…they were the tippy top of a really lousy day."

"What's going on?" Eden took a bite of the pie. "Mmm…this is so good."

"I thought I was doing okay. I mean, all year I've dealt with losing Aaron. I went to a grief counselor. She helped me understand things about my marriage that allowed me to move forward."

"I know." She nodded reassuringly.

"I was doing better. I mean, I finally feel like my life is getting back on track."

"You've got your own place, and everyone's raving about your baked goods." Eden licked the whipped cream off her fork.

"But something happened I didn't expect."

"Is this about your in-laws? You didn't tell me how the visit went."

"Kind of." It would be easier if she could blame her problems on them, but it wouldn't be fair. This mess was her own fault. Did she dare confide in Eden? "Their visit went fine. But my life has changed since Aaron died. I've changed. I think they saw it, too."

"As Gabby is always telling me, change doesn't have to be bad."

"I'm afraid this change is bad." She lowered her eyelids. "I'm attracted to Judd."

"And?" Eden leaned forward, almost spilling her coffee.

Shame rushed over her from head to toe. "And I don't want to be."

"How attracted are we talking?"

*Very.*

*Extremely.*

*More than...*

*Oh, no! I love him!*

*Completely. Utterly. Love. Him.*

This was even worse than she'd thought.

Covering her face with her hands, she tried to hold back the tears. Eden came over to sit next to her.

"It's okay. You haven't done anything wrong."

"I have." Her hands dropped to her lap. "I hurt him. We've been having suppers together most weeknights, and I helped him make Gretchen this gingerbread house—it's so beautiful, Eden—and we just get along. He's easy to be with. And I like hearing about his day. He thinks I'm a good cook. He actually asks about my baking. He helps with the babies. He's so good with them. I can't tell you how wonderful he is."

"Nicole?" Eden gave her shoulder a squeeze. "Are you sure this is only attraction?"

"No." She pinched the bridge of her nose. "It's more. And that's why I hate myself. What kind of person am I? Who does that? Who falls for a guy when their husband died exactly a year ago?"

"Your heart doesn't have a timetable. I mean, love happens when it happens."

"It shouldn't. It's not supposed to. What would people think? What would they say?" She shook her head. "I know what they'd say. 'Oh, that's a Boone girl for you. Just like her mother. Always after a man.' I can't believe I've been so stupid."

"What are you talking about? Everyone

loves your mom," Eden said. "And this is different. It's not as if you've moved in with Judd."

"And I'm never going to." She shifted to face Eden. "I drew a clear line today. I feel terrible, but it was the right thing to do. Judd and I won't be having suppers together anymore. We're not even on speaking terms."

"Are you sure that's what you want?"

She nodded. But it wasn't what she wanted. Not at all.

"Have you prayed about it?" Eden asked.

Of course, she hadn't prayed about it. Well, she had briefly, but not in depth. What could she say? *Hey, God, guess what? I'm an idiot and fell in love again. Only this time it's ridiculously soon after my husband died. Oh, and after You gave me triplets. Proud of me?*

"How does Judd feel about you?" Eden asked.

"Not good." She'd hurt him so badly. And he'd stayed. Helped her. Took care of the babies even after she'd ended things with him. What kind of man did that?

One she didn't deserve.

"I've never seen him take anyone to Christmas Fest." Eden seemed to be talking to herself. "In fact, it's been years since he's even gone to Christmas Fest. He keeps to himself."

"We went together because the church ladies forced us to go."

"Judd? He's not one to be forced into anything." Eden tapped a finger against her chin. "Gretchen's been trying to set him up with women for years, and he's never let her."

This wasn't helping Nicole feel any better.

"After Mia died," Eden said, "it took me a long time to find normal. I know you aren't mad at God for taking Aaron—you've made that clear during our support group meetings. Have you considered the possibility that Judd's a blessing from God? Look at Ruth in the Bible. She lost her husband, and no one thought she was terrible for finding a new one."

"It was different back then. She had no way to support herself, and she had a mother-in-law to feed, too."

Eden shrugged. "You have triplets to support and no family around to help you."

"My in-laws want to help." Nicole sighed. "They asked me to move to Oklahoma. Don't worry. I'm staying here. Besides, lots of people help me."

"What if Judd feels the same for you that you do for him?"

He liked her. Nicole wasn't stupid. But if he felt the same as she did?

Today would be even worse than she'd thought. Because she was in love with the man. And if he loved her, too, she'd taken a sledgehammer to his heart.

"Then I'll never forgive myself."

Eden looked like she wanted to say something, but she simply sighed as if she understood.

That made one of them.

Nicole doubted she'd ever understand how she could have messed up so badly.

"What in the world is this?" Aunt Gretchen opened her storm door. Judd carried the gingerbread house, draped with a tablecloth over it, inside later that night. He could have waited until tomorrow, but if he spent one more minute in his big empty house, he would lose his mind. Tonight he needed to be with someone who loved him.

Aunt Gretchen was the only person he could truly count on.

"Sorry I'm tracking snow inside," he called over his shoulder as he headed straight to her formal dining room to set the house on her table. Once it safely landed, he stepped back, wiped his forehead and returned to the hallway to take off his coat and boots.

Today had been so bad. And the worst part was he had no one to blame but himself.

"I got worried when I didn't see you in church." She hovered near him.

He bent to kiss her cheek. "I should have called you."

"It's okay. It just wasn't like you to miss the Christmas Eve service. Have you eaten?"

"Yeah," he lied. "Want to open your Christmas gift?"

"Is that what this is? It's so big." She circled the table. "I can't imagine what it might be."

He lifted the tablecloth off the house and stood back. The house didn't appear any worse for wear. Then he turned his attention to Aunt Gretchen.

*Please, God, let something go right today. Let her love it.*

Her hands covered her mouth, and her eyes filled with tears. She stared at the house, shaking her head, then looked at him.

"I can't believe it." Sounding breathless, she inspected it closely. "It's just like the house I grew up in. And you did all this?"

"Nicole did most of it." Saying her name

was like a knife to his heart. "I was more for moral support."

Aunt Gretchen peered at the house closely, exclaiming over all of the tiny details. She looked astonished. "I just can't believe it. This is the most thoughtful gift. Oh, Judd, I'm tickled to death."

She flung her arms around him and hugged him tightly. He hugged her back. "I'm glad you like it. I wanted to give you something special. You've been like a mother to me. I love you." He almost choked on the words. He meant them a thousand times over.

"Oh, look at me, crying like a baby." Her smile beamed as tears dropped to her cheeks. "I love you, too. I don't have children, but I couldn't have had a better son than you. You bless me every day, Judd."

She turned her attention back to the house, oohing and aahing over the roof and the porch. Finally, she stood back. "I've got to text your father a picture of this. He'll flip. He always loved that house, too."

Judd doubted it, but it was up to her. She could do what she wanted.

"By the way," he said, "Stu made the wood block it's sitting on. He's really good at woodworking."

She blushed. "Yes, he is. Stu's a good man." She snapped a picture of the house and texted it to his dad. "There. How about some tea and cookies?"

His stomach grumbled.

She chuckled. "Coming right up."

Several minutes later, he held a cup of tea as he sat on her couch. Christmas music played from a speaker somewhere, and Aunt Gretchen nibbled on a frosted sugar cookie shaped like a star.

"I can always tell when something's wrong with you, you know." She raised her eyebrows. "What's going on?"

He might as well be honest with her. She was the only person who seemed to get him.

"I've gotten close to Nicole."

"Oh, good." She set her teacup down.

"I like her. And those babies. They are so sweet."

"It's not good. She's still grieving her husband."

"Give her time, honey. Grief comes and goes."

"Eh." He averted his eyes. "It's not only that. I'm…me."

"What do you mean, you're you? Of course you're you." She sounded indignant.

"I'm too quiet. Too reserved. Too into ranching."

"Did Nicole say that?" Aunt Gretchen sounded huffy.

"No, but I don't know what women want. And I really don't know what Nicole needs."

"Aren't you being a little hard on yourself?"

"I don't think I am."

"What if she's perfect for you?"

He frowned. "I'm not perfect for her."

"Says who?"

*Says me.*

"Judd, you are quiet. You are reserved. You are into ranching. But God made you all those things. Those are good qualities to have."

He was wrong. His aunt was blind as a bat when it came to him.

"He also made you honest, kind, dependable. Genuine. A man who looks after widows like me and widows like Nicole. That's uncommon today."

"I want to look after you."

"I know. And I love you for it."

He wanted to believe her about God making him the way he was, but honestly, it made him kind of mad.

"I wish God could have made me a little more outgoing." He shifted his jaw. "I'm starting to want things I didn't care about before."

"Like a wife? And family?"

"Yes." He practically growled.

"And Nicole isn't ready." Her sympathetic gaze about undid him.

"She made it pretty clear she'll never be ready." When he thought about the envelope with the cash…he balled his hands into fists. How could he have been so stupid?

A soft smile played on her lips. "I wouldn't be so sure about that. I've seen her with you. I've spent many mornings with her and the triplets. She likes you, Judd."

The hope flaming to life was too much to bear.

"I don't think so. It's too complicated. She's not over Aaron."

"Hmm…" Gretchen picked up her teacup again. "I remember the one-year anniversary of my husband's death. I was sure life would never get better. All I could think about was the future we'd never have. But at the time, I didn't realize how life moves on and we move with it. Nicole is probably pretty confused right now. Let her get through Christmas."

It would be great if Aunt Gretchen was right, but he didn't think she was.

"I've been praying for you." She smiled above the rim of the teacup. "I always pray for you. But I have a feeling Nicole moved in to your cabin for a reason."

Yeah, to break his heart.

"Maybe God will listen to your prayers," he said. *He certainly hasn't been listening to mine.* But was that true? Judd hadn't exactly prayed over the situation. In fact, he hadn't prayed about his relationship with Nicole at all.

"Keep asking, keep searching, keep knocking, honey. God wants nothing less."

"I will." His aunt tended to be right.

"And I will, too."

Nicole hauled herself out of bed at four in the morning. She hadn't slept at all. After Eden left, Nicole had stuck the gifts she'd wrapped for the babies under the tree. Then she'd moped for a while. In bed she'd tossed and turned for hours. And now she was plain sick of herself.

Her fluffy robe called to her from the closet. She shuffled over and put it on. In all the fretting of last night, she'd avoided the one thing she should have been doing.

Praying.

Her prayers didn't usually result in instant answers. But when she prayed, she could trust she'd be led to God's will. And she usually felt peace about it.

She plugged in the lights of the Christmas tree and sat on the couch, tucking her legs to the side. Where should she start? Her mind went blank.

How about remembering what Christmas was all about?

*Dear Jesus, it's Christmas again. First, I want to thank You for saving me, a sinner. I wish I was more in the Christmas spirit, but I'm not.*

The colored lights on the tree took the edge off her blues. She had much to be thankful for.

*Thank You for my babies, for keeping us all healthy and for this cabin. I love this cabin. You gave back baking to me and provided an income with it. Thank You for my friends and the women who generously give their time to help me every weekday.*

She wanted to thank Him for Judd, but she wasn't ready. Anxiety gave her the jitters. Swiping through her phone, she opened a Bible app and read a psalm. But it didn't help.

*Lord, I hate feeling this way. Can't I skip Christmas this year? I don't want to think about Aaron. I definitely don't want to think about Judd.*

Her stomach wouldn't stop clenching and unclenching.

*Fine. I give up. Here's what's really going on, Lord. I loved Aaron. And maybe it makes me a horrible person, but I don't miss him the way I think I should. Now I see myself and my life differently. I'm sad, but I'm also looking forward to my future. I feel so guilty. Shouldn't I be mourning still?*

The ticktock of the clock on the wall kept her company as she pushed away the other thoughts. But they kept coming.

*I don't know what to do about Judd. He makes me feel...special. In a way I've never experienced, not even with Aaron.*

*I'm so comfortable with him. What I feel for him is so different from what I felt for Aaron.*

She thought of the dark stairway her grief counselor talked about and the side door with the glowing exit sign next to it.

Her worries about what people around town thought were down the stairwell, along with her in-laws' opinions and her guilt about being disloyal to a dead man.

But what was out the side door?

Something Eden said last night came to mind. *After Mia died, it took me a long time to find normal.*

Maybe that was what was bothering her.

It hadn't taken Nicole long at all to find normal.

As soon as she'd moved in to this cabin, she'd found it.

And Judd was part of her normal.

She'd been trying to follow unspoken rules her entire life. *Be a good girl. Don't be like Mom. Devote your life to Aaron. Pour everything into the babies. Ignore your feelings. You're in mourning.*

Everyone else followed the rules.

She'd supported Aaron through basketball, his diagnosis, college and his career because he'd protected her as a kid and she was too afraid of what her life would look like without him.

But now? The fear of making it on her own was gone. God would always provide a way. Look at what He'd already done in her life.

She'd met her future spouse in second grade, only dated him, then had gotten married at eighteen. She became a widow at twenty-five when she was pregnant with triplets.

Forget *everyone else*—she'd never even been like *anyone* else.

The glowing exit sign in her mind beckoned. If she opened the side door, she knew what she would find. Three happy babies. A thriving home baking business. Good friends. And a quiet, handsome cowboy named Judd.

The future was full of sunshine and cupcakes. If she was willing to go for it.

All of her anxiety dissolved, and she was left with a strange peace. She couldn't explain it. She felt empty. In a good way.

She'd gotten through the worst year of her life.

And she was ready to embrace the future she wanted.

Judd drove the tractor to feed the herd as the sun peeked over the horizon Christmas morning. Large snowflakes danced to the ground. His cows followed the line of feed, munching and enjoying their Christmas spread. To him it was a day like most others. Except he'd wadded up his heart last night and left it on his back porch for the wild animals to scavenge.

Aunt Gretchen's words had given him hope, but what good was hope? It would only get trampled down like the hay the cattle stomped on as they ate.

Avoiding Nicole would be hard. He already missed holding the babies. He couldn't stand the idea of not seeing Nicole's smiling face across the table each evening. He didn't even look forward to the thought of not having to make conversation. He actually *liked* making conversation with her.

Last night before bed, he'd tried to pray, but he couldn't find the right words. He didn't know what he wanted to say. Leave it to him to not even be able to string the right words together in his head to tell the Lord.

Maybe he should try again.

*God, I'm sorry I'm not good at praying. I wish You'd give Nicole what she needs. I realize that's not me. All year I've thought about her and enjoyed her company. And these past few weeks...well, that woman and the triplets have become my world.*

He stared out at the white pastures before him. This ranch had been his whole world for twenty years.

The land and cattle had been enough before. They would have to be enough now.

When the hay was distributed, he turned around and headed back to the barn. A few of the cows looked up at him and mooed as he passed by.

"Merry Christmas to you, too," he yelled.

After parking the tractor, he went to the stables to feed the horses and let them out. Candy's ears pricked up as she nudged her nose at him.

"Love you, too, Candy Cane." He petted her nose and neck, then gave her an apple. "Merry Christmas."

He led her and Diesel and the other horses out to the pasture. They tossed their heads in the air as the snow fell. Propping his boot on the lowest fence rail, he watched them enjoy the weather.

When the chill crept into his bones, he pushed away from the fence and strode to the house. After a quick shower, he poured a mug of coffee and sat in his living room, staring at the tall blue spruce he'd chopped down and decorated a few weeks ago.

Today would be tough on Nicole. He didn't like to think of her crying alone with the babies on Christmas Day. But she didn't want him around.

From the corner of his eye, the presents he'd bought her and the babies came into view. Maybe he should stop over there quick. To check on her. Give her the presents. Then he'd leave her alone for good.

*Why?*

He frowned. *Why what? Why go over there or why leave her alone for good?*

A spurt of adrenaline made his pulse leap.

Yesterday Nicole had told him Aaron was her whole life. And not an hour ago while feeding the cows, Judd had thought this ranch was *his* whole life.

But his life had expanded to include her. And her children.

And after Aaron had died, Nicole's had expanded to include three babies.

Was it possible her life could expand to include him, too?

He hopped to his feet, causing the coffee to slosh out of his mug down his hand. He went to the kitchen and wiped it off with a paper towel.

He'd always assumed the qualities that had kept him from falling in love and getting married were bad. That for whatever reason he wasn't equipped for love or marriage.

But maybe those qualities were the ones Nicole needed.

Was it possible he'd never fallen in love or gotten married because he was meant to love her?

He had something to give her that no one else could.

His complete devotion.

Aunt Gretchen was right. Nicole needed time to grieve and work through her loss. But Judd had another quality many others lacked.

Patience.

He'd wait for her as long as it took.

He was meant for Nicole, and she was meant for him. He wasn't going to settle for anything less, even if it took twenty years for her to come around.

# *Chapter Fifteen*

Nicole wrapped a fuzzy scarf around her neck at dawn. She'd fallen into a deep sleep for two hours, gotten up, showered and put on a soft sweater with her favorite leggings. The sun had just risen, and large snowflakes fell outside. It was still too early for the babies to wake up. She needed to make peace with her past before they did.

With the baby monitor in her pocket and warm boots on her feet, she slipped out to the front porch.

Beautiful. Snow spread like frosting on the branches of the evergreen trees. The lane leading to Judd's house could have been made of whipped cream. A cardinal flew between the trees. A perfect Christmas morning. The silent atmosphere gave her the strength she needed.

"Aaron, I know you can't hear me, but I want you to know I'm okay," she said quietly to the air. "The babies are getting big, and they're healthy. Eli looks just like you. He'll be a handsome boy, like his daddy." Her lips trembled. "I lost you last year. One year ago today. And I thought my life was over. I couldn't imagine experiencing anything good again after you died."

She swallowed the huge lump in her throat.

"It's been hard." Her voice cracked. "I've had to fight anxiety. It's tried to sink me again and again. Even last night. It's getting easier to fight it, though."

A breeze showered sparkly snowflakes on the porch rail.

"I've met someone. A guy. A cowboy, really. He's a good man. An honorable one. He loves your babies. You wouldn't believe how tender he is with them. I know you don't want to hear this. I know it would hurt you to find out I've moved on, so I want you to be the first to know. I *am* moving on. I want to. God gave me a second chance, and I'm taking it."

The guilt that had been weighing her down for so long flew away as easily as a butterfly in the spring.

"Goodbye, Aaron. Till we meet again." She closed her eyes and tilted her face upward. The release was bittersweet, but she knew it was right.

She needed to make something else right, too. She had to apologize to Judd and thank him for taking care of her and the babies yesterday after she'd treated him so badly.

Most of all, she had to tell him she was wrong.

Their connection was real, it was deep and it was special.

She'd do anything to protect it.

Nicole was going to invite him over and lay out her heart to him. He might not want it. Yesterday might have killed any chances she had with him. But she had to try.

If the town thought she was like her mom, oh, well. She finally understood the difference between them. Her mom latched on to any man. And only one would do for Nicole.

Maybe he should call her. Or text her.

Judd stood on his porch with a shopping bag full of presents in one hand and a small wrapped box in his coat pocket. He'd put on a nice button-down shirt with dark jeans. His Stetson protected his hair from the snow, and while his cowboy boots weren't as practical as his snow boots, they were a part of him, and he needed every ounce of confidence he could muster.

He, Judd Wilson, was going to tell Nicole exactly how he felt.

He wanted her to know what was on his mind. And if she still cut him out of her life? It would be the hardest thing he could imagine, but he'd get through it with the Lord's help.

*Just one step, man. The first step is always the hardest.*

He moved forward, then marched down the porch. No UTV today. He needed time to figure out what to say. His stomach wasn't great. It had tied itself into knots and seemed to be trying to work itself free.

Gritting his teeth, he continued down her lane. Rays of sunshine streamed onto the snow, giving everything a shimmer it usually lacked.

What if he got to the door and she wouldn't let him in? What if someone else was there?

He hadn't thought this through. But the bend in the lane brought her cabin into view, and he had to admit, it did look dropped out of a fairy tale. The roof dripped with snow, and smoke wreathed out of the chimney.

And there, on the porch, stood Nicole. She had a big scarf wrapped around her neck, and her eyes were closed. He took long strides, his heart racing, the grip on the bag tightening as he made his way up the steps to join her on the porch.

"Oh, Judd, I can't believe you're here." She made it sound like it was a good thing. "I'm so sorry for yesterday. When I think about how awful I was—" she shook her head, averting her eyes "—it almost makes me sick."

He wished she would clarify. Was she sorry for the whole rent thing or for crying? He set the bag down and moved to stand in front of her.

"I'm sorry I insulted you by giving you rent. I'd like to tell you my intentions were good, but they weren't. I was scared."

"You don't have to be scared of me." His voice was low and scratchy.

"Not of you. Of this." She pointed to him and back to herself. "I felt so guilty that I was growing close to you when Aaron hasn't even been gone a year. I didn't want to be like my mother. Her advice to me usually involves snagging a man."

His lips twitched upward at the last part.

Her eyelashes lowered. "But the thing I feared the most was needing you."

"You need me?" His throat was as parched as the prairie in August. Bone-dry.

She nodded, lifting those sage-green eyes to his. "I didn't want to need anyone. I'd spent most of my life needing Aaron. I wanted to be independent. Wanted to make it on my own."

"You *are* independent."

"Judd, I have three infants. I'm living here for free. The ladies from church help me five days a week. I am as far from independent as I've ever been."

"You're not a charity case." He clenched his hands to keep from reaching out and touching her. "Everyone likes you and wants to help out. Is that why you wanted to pay me rent? Do I make you feel dependent? Or incapable or something?"

"No." She took a step closer. He felt woozy all of a sudden. She smelled like sugar cookies. "You don't. And that's not why I tried to pay you rent. I was scared of my feelings."

He wanted to touch her. Put his arms around her. Reassure her.

"You mean a lot to me," she said. "Too much, really." She turned to look at the trees, then faced him again. "You're the reason I went to events when I first moved back. If I knew you'd be at a barbecue or social function, I didn't have to worry about falling apart. Sitting by you calmed me. I didn't have to talk. We could just sit there and be together."

He'd never realized his presence could comfort someone. He'd always felt like an awkward bump on a log.

"And when Mom told me she was moving, the girls urged me to talk to you about renting this cabin. I hadn't been that nervous in a long time."

"I wanted you to have it."

"I know. But even then I was aware I was attracted to you. I worried… Well, I worried about falling for you."

"You were attracted to me?" His chest swelled. He moved closer to her.

"Yeah."

"I thought I was too old for you."

"Why would you think that?"

He shrugged. Hope danced around his heart.

"Anyway, I…" Her expression grew melancholy. "It was kind of you—so kind—to take care of me and the babies yesterday. Especially after…"

The hope building inside him crashed to the ground. Was that it? She apologized and…nothing?

Rejection dripped in. Maybe it was best to walk away and lick his wounds. It was what he would have done in the past.

*Not this time. Are you a cowboy or a coward?*

Nicole was being honest with him. She'd allowed him a glimpse inside her heart. And he owed her the same.

The words stuck like burrs in his throat. What could he say to make her understand?

*Lord, I need Your help here.*

"I wanted to take care of you and the babies," he blurted out. "I take care of everything on my ranch."

Was that all she was to him? Something on his ranch to take care of?

Nicole's core hollowed out with a whoosh. Judd straightened, looking powerful and in control. For a few minutes there, she'd thought maybe he loved her, too. But now she wasn't so sure.

"I like sitting by you at barbecues and things like that," he said gruffly. "I wasn't keen on having supper together every night when you first mentioned it."

Perfect. He hated their suppers together.

"But I balked because I liked you. A lot. And I thought it was inappropriate to have those kinds of feelings for a beautiful woman like yourself. I mean, you had your hands full with three babies and recently lost the man you loved. It didn't cross my mind that I stood a chance with you."

Her heart began to sing like the birds in the trees.

"Plus, if you haven't noticed, I'm not much of a talker, and I figured you'd be bored to death after two meals."

She couldn't help herself—she laughed. His smile was bright, and his eyes had never looked so warm and inviting.

"You never bore me, Judd."

"Well, you couldn't bore me, Nicole. I could spend every evening with you, talking or in complete silence, and I'd be content. You're something special. And I know you're grieving. I know today's a hard, hard day for you. I don't want to add to it. But I've got gifts for the little ones. And I've got a present for you."

She shivered from the cold.

"You're freezing. Let's go inside. You need to warm up." He put his arm around her and directed her indoors. "I'll pour you a cup of coffee. Go. Sit down."

Moments later, she accepted a steaming mug from him. He sat next to her on the couch, his thigh brushing hers. Then he handed her a rectangular box wrapped in candy-striped paper.

After setting the mug on the end table, she took the present and stared into his eyes with a million unasked questions.

He nodded. "Go ahead."

She tore off the paper and tossed it to the side. A blue jewelry box. Her breath caught. Slowly, she opened it. And gasped.

A silver chain held three silver bars. The babies' names were engraved on them.

"I figured your husband would have gotten you something like this if he would have lived."

She covered her mouth with her hand. The gesture was so beautiful, so thoughtful—so Judd.

"Are you okay?" He caressed her cheek.

"More than okay." Her voice trembled. "Will you put it on for me?"

She pulled her hair over her shoulder and turned her back to him. His fingers grazed her neck as he clasped the necklace. Then she turned around and hugged him.

"Thank you. Judd, this is above anything I could have imagined. I don't deserve it. I don't deserve you."

His hands pressed her closer, and he whispered in her ear. "You deserve more."

She jerked back and stared into his eyes. "Don't say that. You're everything I want in a man, and I bring so much baggage."

"If the baggage you're referring to is three little babies, I'll gladly help you with it."

"It is." She could stare into his eyes forever. "But it's more than that. After Aaron's death, well, I have anxiety sometimes."

"Understandable."

"This cabin helps. Spending time with you *really* helps."

"It does?" He brushed her hair behind her ear. "I guess we should spend more time together, then. I'd like to date you. Court you. I'm not in a rush."

"Dating?" she said breathlessly. She could picture them holding hands, going out to dinner, spending time together. Just them. "In some ways, Aaron and I were an old married couple by the time we were thirteen years old."

"Well, I haven't dated much, and I've definitely never felt like an old married couple at any point in my life. So I guess this will be new for both of us."

"I guess so." She beamed at him. "This is probably too soon, but I want to say it."

"What?" The pulse in his neck was beating fast.

"I love you," she said.

His throat worked as he took her hand and kissed the back of it.

"I love you, too." He held it to his heart and leaned in to kiss her.

When his lips pressed against hers, she said a silent prayer, thanking God. He pulled her close to him, and she got lost in the strength of his arms, the warmth of his body, the sweetness of his lips.

She was ready for this. Ready for Judd Wilson. Ready to love again.

Squeaks and coos crackled through the baby monitor in her pocket.

Judd broke away from the kiss and grinned. “Guess who’s up?”

“They can wait a few minutes.” She tugged him back to her.

“I’m not arguing with that.”

Neither was she.

# Chapter Sixteen

"I can't believe our friends did all this." Nicole shook her head in wonder.

Judd took the stack of used paper plates out of her hand and threw them in the trash. They were alone in her kitchen for the moment. One by one, their friends had been stopping by all day. Eden had brought presents and a plate of cheese and crackers at noon. Mason and Brittany, his brother, Ryder, and all three of their kids came a little later, bearing a platter of sliced ham and a box of chocolates. Then Dylan, Gabby and her daughter, Phoebe, drove up at four with biscuits and a basket of jellies.

He'd called Aunt Gretchen earlier to let her know he was spending all day with Nicole and the triplets. She'd been concerned about them eating a proper Christmas meal, so she'd proceeded to bring the entire Christmas dinner along with Stu to Nicole's cabin. His aunt and Stu had helped with the babies all afternoon. In fact, they were the only guests remaining.

Nicole and Aunt Gretchen had discussed the gingerbread house at length, and there'd been hugs and more than one round of happy tears. Every time Judd looked at them, he loved his aunt even more. He could only guess she would encourage Nicole the way she'd done with him for so many years.

Judd's parents had even called. His dad had gone on and on about the gingerbread house being just like the house he'd grown up in. They'd had a good conversation for once, and Judd had been shocked when

Dad told him they were flying out to Wyoming to visit in February.

"Well, Stu, I think it's time we got out of their hair." Aunt Gretchen patted his knee and rose from the couch. "It's been a lovely Christmas. Thank you for letting us spend it with you and these dear babies."

His aunt bent over to say goodbye to the triplets spelling out Ho, Ho, Ho in the outfits he'd given them while Stu gathered the coats. Judd and Nicole followed them to the door. Out on the porch, Stu took Aunt Gretchen's arm and helped her down to the sidewalk. She smiled up at him, and he kissed her cheek.

The sight warmed Judd's heart. Both he and his aunt had found someone special for Christmas.

Judd had finally gotten the Christmas-movie ending he'd always dreamed about.

He slowly shut the door. "My aunt has a boyfriend."

"I know. They are the cutest couple ever." Nicole slid her arm around him and leaned her cheek against his side.

"They are pretty cute." He kissed the top of her head.

"I've been dreading this day for so long, but it's been incredible."

"I'm glad."

Her phone rang. "Oh, it's Mom. I've got to take this."

"Go ahead." He returned to the living area and knelt down to talk to the babies.

"Merry Christmas, Nicki!"

"Merry Christmas to you, too. How's Steve?"

Judd didn't mean to eavesdrop, but he paused when he heard his own name. "Yes, Judd is good. In fact, he's here with me now… Uh-huh. Yeah. Actually, Mom, we're going to start dating."

An excited squeal came through the phone, and Nicole held her phone away from her ear as she turned to stare at Judd. Her eyes widened in amused surprise. "Okay, okay, I will. You, too. Merry Christmas."

She hung up, came over and got on her knees next to him.

"Mom's pretty happy. She likes you."

"Good." He grinned her way. "I wouldn't want her to worry."

Her fingers touched the necklace. "It doesn't matter what anyone thinks. We were meant to be together. Oh, I forgot to tell you. I'm naming my baking business Triply Sweet. What do you think?"

"I think it's perfect." He kissed her cheek. "You and these babies have made my life triply sweet."

## *Epilogue*

Getting evicted by her own mother turned out to be the best thing that could have happened to Nicole. She stood in the doorway of the converted barn where Gabby and Dylan's wedding reception was winding down as she watched for Judd's truck to pull up. The early-April weather had stayed dry but cool for the wedding.

It had been a beautiful ceremony. Eden was the maid of honor, and Brittany and Nicole were bridesmaids. Judd, Mason and Ryder had all been groomsmen, and Stu Miller was the best man. Gretchen, Lois and Jane took care of the triplets during the ceremony. Then Judd and Nicole had taken the children back to her cabin, where they'd hired three high school girlfriends to babysit during the reception.

Stu and Gretchen had danced next to her and Judd at the reception. They were such a sweet couple. They truly appreciated each other.

Maybe it was a case of wedding feels, but Nicole couldn't help longing for a wedding of her own. She and Judd had gotten even closer since Christmas. They still ate supper together every night. Most Saturdays they hired the three high school girls to babysit the triplets so they could go on a date. At nine months old, the babies were happy, playful and very energetic. They were already crawling and getting into everything. She had no idea how she was going to keep up with them. Judd helped a lot.

All the dating and courting had been a dream come true.

But Nicole was ready for something more.

Judd's truck stopped in front of the entrance, and he got out. Nicole's mouth went dry seeing him in his tuxedo. Naturally, he wore a cowboy hat with it. Only made him that much more appealing. She went outside to join him.

"Have I told you how beautiful you look?" He put his arms around her waist and bent to look in her eyes. She shivered in anticipation.

"Yes. About fifty times." She playfully pushed against his chest. "You can say it fifty more. I won't get tired of it."

"Good, because you take my breath away." He kissed her cheek, stepped back and took her by the hand. "Come on. Let's get out of here."

They chatted about the wedding all the way back to his ranch, and then he parked in front of his house.

"Wait. Aren't you forgetting something?" she asked.

"What?"

"I live down there." She pointed to the lane leading to the cabin.

"I know. This is a slight detour." He held

up his index finger. "Let me come around and help you out. I have something inside for you."

What was this all about? She tried to imagine what he was up to, but she couldn't. Her pulse sped up as he opened the door and helped her down.

His eyes darkened with appreciation as his gaze took her in from head to toe. Her red dress was a bit more daring than the high necklines she usually wore, but Gabby had chosen the bridesmaids' dresses. And Judd seemed to like it.

They walked up his porch steps, and he ushered her inside, where he led her to his living room. A few dim lamps glowed. Her heart swelled and thumped.

He lit a few candles. He looked handsome and mysterious and…nervous.

"This looks romantic." She loved his house.

"I hope so." He brought her to the center of the room. "These past months have been incredible."

"I agree." Her heart was acting funny, like a car trying to sputter to life.

"Courting has been a dream come true, and I'll date you as long as you'll have me."

"I feel the same way." Her heart swelled. Was Judd getting ready to propose? *Please, God, let him be ready!*

"I hope this isn't too soon." He lowered himself to one knee. "But I'm not getting any younger. I'm ready for more. I'm ready for forever. Nicole Taylor, will you marry me?"

He held out a square box and opened it, revealing a diamond ring inside.

"Oh, Judd..." She touched her lips. "Yes! I want to marry you. I'm ready for forever, too."

"You mean it? You'll marry me?"

"I've been ready to marry you for a while, cowboy."

He rose and hauled her into his arms, lifting her off her toes as he spun her around. Then he slowly slid her back to her feet and kissed her. The promise of his devotion was in his kiss. When he ended it, he looked into her eyes and smiled. "Want to try the ring on?"

"Yes!" She admired it as he slid it on her finger. "You didn't have to buy me the biggest diamond in Rendezvous."

"I wanted to, Nicole. You're…everything to me." His eyes smoldered as he kissed the back of her hand.

"I feel the same about you, Judd." She bit her lower lip. "Are you sure you're up for triplets?"

"You know I love them. I'm even up for more if you're game."

"Give me a few years."

He laughed, wrapping his arms around her waist. "I guess everyone was right."

"About what?" Putting her arms around his neck, she looked into the face of the man she loved. How could she have been this blessed?

"My long-term plan needed a wife and kids."

"It really did. In fact, it might need a pet, too. I'd like to get a kitten eventually."

"A kitten, huh? I think I can handle that."

"You're too good to me, Judd."

"You're the best thing that's ever happened to me."

"Well, I guess that makes us a team."

"Team Wilson."

"Forever."

* * * * *

*If you enjoyed this*
*Wyoming Sweethearts book by*
*Jill Kemerer, be sure to*
*pick up the previous*
*books in this miniseries:*

Her Cowboy Till Christmas
The Cowboy's Secret

*Available now from Love Inspired!*

Dear Reader,

What is it about tiny babies and big, strong cowboys? My heart melts every time. I have to admit I was nervous about writing this book. I worried readers wouldn't understand how Nicole could make the leap from grieving widow to ready to love again in just under a year. But as the story developed, the simple truth came through. Love has its own timetable for each of us.

Nicole's life had never followed a regular path, and it was okay for her to accept that. She didn't need to spend the rest of her life alone. Having a future with Judd could never erase the years she had with Aaron. As for Judd, he's such a great guy. Humble, trustworthy, dependable—I fell in love with him from chapter one. I'm glad he found a woman who truly appreciates him.

And now I want to make one of those gorgeous gingerbread houses! The one time I attempted to make a gingerbread house, it was a sloppy mess. It's probably best if I stick to looking at other people's masterpieces.

I love connecting with readers. Feel free to email me at jill@jillkemerer.com or write me at PO Box 2802, Whitehouse, Ohio, 43571.

May your Christmas season be filled with joy!

Merry Christmas,
*Jill Kemerer*